THE NECROMANCER
THROUGH THE VEIL

Stacey Oakley

THE NECROMANCER by Stacey Oakley
Book 1 of Through the Veil

ISBN: 978-7750407-2-9

Cover design by Stacey Oakley

Cover images from Unsplash users Ryan Card and Alexandru Zdrobău

Cover font is Demons & Darlings by Chad Savage

Written in Canada by Stacey Oakley

Printed internationally by IngramSpark

Visit writershaunt.wordpress.com

To my readers.
I couldn't do this without you.

I

"Do I have to go?" The boy asked, even as he tried to pull his arm from her grip. He seemed surprised that she still held on. That was fair, since there weren't many people who could hold onto a ghost.

"I'm afraid so. You don't belong here anymore," Cora replied, her tone gentle despite the wild goose chase she'd been led on through downtown St John's, and the fact that this was the last case of a very long day. He couldn't have been more than seven or eight when he died, and souls didn't really age past that point. So, despite having been dead for about a hundred years, he was still just a kid.

"Where 'm I gonna go?"

"That's above my pay grade, buddy." Not even reapers like her, who could occasionally cross the Veil, knew what really happened to souls after they passed on. She considered it to be between the person and whatever they worshipped, but she decided against saying that now. It might just confuse the kid more. "But maybe there'll be other people waiting for you." It was hard with children. The unknown was scary, and they had to face it all alone.

"Like Mom and Dad? And me sister, Jenny?" He seemed excited for a moment, but then his expression fell. "But none of them talked to me, and they all left me behind when they died too. I tried to talk to 'em. They talked about me lots, but they couldn't see me."

"Well, you know that most people can't normally see ghosts, now. So, they probably just didn't know you were around, and they thought they'd see you on the other side." She hoped she wasn't lying to him. She couldn't imagine what that must have been like, to be a child feeling abandoned by the family who didn't know they lingered. Clairvoyants who could see ghosts and Mediums who could see them as well as communicate with those who had passed beyond the vale were uncommon, and reapers were rare. Cora's family were the only reapers in the province and had been since Europeans started settling on the island. Any stories of reapers before them, from the Beothuk people, had been lost a long time ago.

The boy, Jack, nodded. "I miss them."

She nodded. "Do you want to join them?"

He swallowed hard, a reflex that lingered from life, but nodded. "I wanna see them again." But he still looked so scared. "Will it hurt?"

She shook her head. Many ghosts asked that question, and she'd even come to expect it. But when it came from a kid it still got to her. "Its just like walking through curtains. I've done it before."

"Okay."

Still keeping a hold on Jack's hand, she drew her dagger. The Damascus blade was as long as her forearm, ancient runes and symbols etched into the razor-sharp steel. Pieces of blue scapolite were inset into the crossguard and the pommel. She couldn't help but grin when his eyes widened at the sight of it.

"I thought the Grimm Reaper used a scythe," he said.

"Have you held a scythe before? They might look cool, but they are big and *heavy*," she replied, eliciting a small grin from him. "This works a lot better, especially when I have to chase ghosts." On its own the dagger had no magical properties, the etchings more ritual than anything. Once in her hand, however, it could act as an extension of her power. She took a deep breath and focused as she'd been trained to do, feeling for the division between this world and the next. She always thought of it as a silk curtain, and she could feel it brushing over her skin. It was thick and cool, though on Halloween it would be so thin it almost ceased to exist. For now, she carefully set the edge of her blade against it and sliced down, creating an opening that emitted an ethereal grey light.

"So that's where I gotta go?"

She looked down at Jack. "Yup." She didn't put the knife away. Sometimes things came through the Veil that shouldn't.

"Can I have a few more minutes?"

Cora shook her head. "No, because then you'll keep asking for more and putting it off." She'd been there before more than once. Delaying the inevitable just made things harder. "Its time. Your family is waiting, remember?"

"But what if they aren't?" He tried to take a step back. "You don't know what's on the other side."

"Do you really want to stay here? It doesn't seem like much fun." She didn't want to have to force him through. "There'll be others there, they'll all be able to see you, and you can find someone to play with. Its time, Jack."

"Can you come with me? You said you've been through before."

"Not this time, sorry. But you can do it. Its time." She tried to nudge him forward. He resisted initially, but he did move. "You're brave. Not many ghosts can give a reaper a chase like you did." That gave him a glimmer of pride. "Now go on. I'll be right here until you go through." No matter how unfair it was that his life had been cut short so young.

Jack nodded, and she let go of him. "Okay." He went through the motions of taking a deep breath, then slowly went up to the portal. He paused to look back at her. "Will you remember me? I don't think anyone else does."

"I will," she promised. "Like I said, not many ghosts can outrun me for so long." And if she hadn't had to deal with a borderline poltergeist haunting earlier, the chase would have been much shorter.

Satisfied, he went through the tear and vanished into the soft grey light. Her throat felt oddly tight as she flipped her dagger so that the pommel was at the top of the tear and focused her power, feeling the edges of the rift in the fabric of the world, and ran her other hand over it, like she was smoothing out curtains to make the edges meet. Just like that, it was closed. The little boy had moved on. Cora took a deep breath and leaned back against the wall of a building for a moment, gathering herself. She hated dealing with ghost children. Everyone did. But it had to be done. It wasn't her first one, hell, it wasn't even the first one of the day, and she knew it wouldn't be the last.

Break over, she pulled out a small notebook she always kept on her and recorded Jack's details so they could update the archives. Her phone went off as she put the notebook away and she checked it, hoping it wasn't something work-related from her brother. She wanted to go home. It wasn't from him, but it *was* a text from Emily, which reminded Cora that she had a date to get ready for. She'd been looking forward to it earlier, but now... it had been a hard day, and Jack was just the finishing touch. She wanted to see Emily, but she also wanted to lie down on the couch, watch terrible horror movies, and drink wine. Getting all dressed up and dealing with crowds... it felt like too much.

Heart heavy, she headed back to her car and started the drive home. If she shed a tear, well, no one was around to see it. In spite of all the training they received and all the support, some days were just like that. Some days were just... heavy. She was dealing with the dead, and sometimes the families of the dead, people terrorized by poltergeists or afraid of ghosts, and people were still afraid of reapers. Everything just piled up and weighed her down.

She was ready to just go home and relax.

Despite the traffic, Cora made it home in good time. She lived just far enough from downtown to have a driveway of her own, which had been one of her main requirements in a house. She owned half a duplex, which was currently painted a cheerful lime green with complementary blue trimming. For now, anyway. Cora's housemate was already talking about changing it. It had been yellow when she'd bought the place a little over a year ago.

As she stepped inside, she checked to see if there were any paint cans by the door, but luckily there weren't. It had become a habit to check. The agreement was that Maryanne could repaint the entire house once a year. She hung up her coat and kicked off her boots before going into the living room and face-planting onto the couch with a groan. She was starting to feel the aches of the day. Jack wasn't the only runner she'd had to deal with. Plus, a ghost who had enjoyed throwing things at her. It felt like playing dodge ball in school again. Except the balls were knives, hardcover books, and anything heavy. That particular ghost had been close to turning into a poltergeist and she'd had to kill her, but given the bruises she was going to end up with in the morning, she didn't feel as bad about that as she could have.

Something most people forgot was that reapers could kill ghosts. Their magic could destroy a soul, erase it from existence. The same thing happened to someone killed on the other side of the veil. No one quite knew what came after, what happened to the soul after a second death.

"Hard day at work?" Maryanne asked. Cora nodded without lifting her head. She was used to her housemate not making a sound. Ghosts tended to be quiet when they moved. "Want to talk about it?"

Cora turned her head so she could look at Maryanne. "A kid, a few people who weren't ready to go, and a fucking nightmare that would be a poltergeist in a week." Unlike most people, dead or alive, Maryanne didn't flinch at the eye contact. White irises ringed in red were a universal marker of reapers, no matter where in the world they were from. Most found it unnerving at best, and with everything else, real or myth, they didn't often stick around to get used to it. Maryanne had never seemed bothered by it, though. She gave Cora a sympathetic look.

"Are you still going on your date tonight?"

"I want too..." But the longer she lay there, the less she wanted to get up. Taking a deep breath, she forced herself to stand. "I will." She dragged herself up to her room and stared into her closet without really seeing her clothes and tried to remember where they were going.

"Cora?"

She turned and looked at Maryanne, whose expression indicated she'd probably been standing and staring longer than she'd meant to. "Sorry, spaced out."

"Its fine... why don't you invite Emily over instead of going out? I can make a nice supper for the two of you and you can relax and watch movies or something instead of dressing up and going out."

That sounded like the best idea she'd heard all day. "But will that bother you?"

She shook her head. "I have some shopping to do and you look like you could use a night in. Besides, I like Emily and your cooking will impress no one."

Ignoring the commentary on her admittedly mediocre culinary skills, she considered it. "What shopping are you doing?" As a ghost Maryanne was stuck wearing the clothes she had died in. She dealt with it by frequently redecorating the spaces around her. She had a great eye for interior design on a budget, so Cora mostly let her do what she wanted. Maryanne had even started something of an online consulting business for interior decorating. Her clients just didn't know they were dealing with a Victorian-era ghost.

It was a little funny that a ghost who had lived in the mid-nineteenth century was so tech-savvy. Even better, ghosts could enhance signals and electricity as well as disrupt it. As a result, they had fantastic internet and all of the channels.

"I need to stage the living room for a winter shoot."

"Its October."

"I know, I'm a bit late. Anyway, do you want to have a date here?"

"Yes. And we're keeping the furniture."

"Oh, that's fine. I can drape fabric over it if I need to."

"And if you do *anything* with glitter, you're cleaning it up." Cora hadn't forgotten the fiasco from last year.

Maryanne raised a brow. "I'm still finding glitter from when you went to Pride."

"That wasn't my fault."

"Sure..."

"It wasn't!"

Maryanne was still clearly unconvinced. "Right."

"I'm calling Emily." It was a useless argument.

"I hold her equally at fault."

"I'll let her know."

"Good." Maryanne drifted out of the room to give her some privacy. Cora took a deep breath as she selected Emily from her contact list, though the argument had helped lighten her mood a little.

She answered quickly. "Hey, we still on for tonight?"

"About that, do you mind if we change our plans? I'm not really feeling up for a fancy dinner tonight... do you want to just come over?" She couldn't help but feel anxious as she asked. They hadn't been together long, only since the start of summer.

"Yeah, that's fine. Hard day at work?" There was no hesitation.

"Yeah..." Emily knew what she was. It wasn't like she could hide it, not without coloured contacts. She'd used them occasionally, when she thought there was a significant risk to her safety, but she hated wearing them and hated putting them in even more.

"If you want, we can get together some other time," she offered.

"I mean, we can if you'd rather go out. I would like to see you, though." It was a fight to keep her voice steady, and she hated it. But experience had taught her that there was always some point where what she was became too much. Too creepy, too depressing, too morbid. Inevitably, she was left with a broken heart. She wasn't alone, a lot of reapers had that problem, but that didn't mean it hurt any less when it happened.

"Okay. Same time?"

"Sounds good."

"Who's cooking?"

"Maryanne."

"Thank God." Cora could almost hear the smile in her voice, and couldn't quite help a small smile of her own.

"Seriously?"

Emily laughed softly. "Don't worry, Cora, you have other talents I enjoy. I'll see you soon."

"Bye," Cora grumbled, though she wasn't really grumpy about it. She sighed in relief and let herself fall back onto her bed. Emily was completely normal. Not a medium, not a clairvoyant, and not a reaper. A totally normal human. She worked with computers. She could only see Maryanne because the longer ghosts stuck around the more energy they absorbed and became stronger, until they were visible to anyone if they wanted to be. Being around reapers gave them an odd boost and helped keep them stable so they didn't become poltergeists. Reapers benefited because there were times when they needed to talk to ghosts, and most were understandably afraid of them. It was a strange and mutually beneficial partnership.

"Well?" The ghost in question drifted back into the room a few moments later.

"She's coming over at seven."

Maryanne smiled. "Perfect. I'll get to work. Why don't you take a nap?"

"If I fall asleep I'm not sure I'll wake up in time," Cora replied in a wry tone. "Do you need any help?"

She considered. "I could use some help cutting things up."

Once again Cora forced herself upright. "Do we have any coffee?"

"Yes, but you're on your own for that."

Cora nodded and quickly changed into comfortable - but still nice- clothes and went downstairs to start a pot of coffee. Maryanne got to work and her often translucent form became opaque as she started cooking, an odd mix of subtle telekineses that was an impressive show of skill and power. It almost looked like she was really touching things. Cora turned her attention back to what she was doing, making very strong coffee and taking a couple ibuprofen to try to get rid of some of the soreness. Too many winces and Emily would probably want to know what happened, which Cora really didn't want to get into. It might risk getting to that 'too much' point sooner. She really liked Emily, and really wanted this to go well.

There was something oddly relaxing about cooking, especially when someone else was doing all of the important work and she didn't actually have to pay attention to anything. Between that and the coffee, she was feeling a little better by the time the doorbell rang, able to muster up a genuine smile as she let Emily in. Emily kissed her as she walked in and shut the door.

"I brought wine," she said, holding up the bottle. "Feeling better?"

"A little," Cora replied, taking it and heading into the kitchen.

"Want to talk about it?" Emily's brown eyes were full of sincere concern.

"Not really." Cora hid her face against Emily's shoulder to hide her grimace, her fears of finding out where the line was remained in the forefront of her mind.

"Okay." Warm arms wrapped around her waist, pulling her close. "Whatever you're cooking smells great, Maryanne."

"Thanks. How are you today?" Most might find it strange that a ghost would use modern inflection. Most didn't. But those who did tended to last longer before turning into a poltergeist or a shade, fading into the kind of ghost that spent its time repeating actions.

"Alright, though some fuckwit at work fell for a scam on a work computer and everyone in my department got to spend the day doing damage control and virus clean up, since he managed to spread it to several other computers." Cora could feel Emily shaking her head. "At least there are four of us here. I was the only IT person at the last company I worked for and it was a nightmare."

"Sounds like it." Cora lifted her head and stepped away to get two wine glasses. She glanced at Emily. "Do you want to stay the night?"

She grinned as she leaned against the counter. "Well, I wouldn't say no."

"Alright, then we can let the wine pour," Cora said, doing just that with a flourish.

"Well, everything is ready, so I'll leave you two for now," Maryanne said, turning off the oven.

"You're not joining us?" Emily wondered, sipping her wine.

"No, not tonight. Enjoy yourselves!" She replied, then went up through the ceiling. Cora couldn't help but laugh at Emily's expression.

"I suppose I should have expected that," she said in a wry tone, shaking her head. "I guess you get used to it."

"Yeah." Cora served up the food. It was a nice dinner, most of it spent debating whether horror movies or horror games were scarier. A few glasses of wine later, they ended up on the couch, flicking through channels to see if anything good was on television.

"Did you see the news last night?" Emily wondered, running her fingers through Cora's hair. Cora was stretched out along the couch, using Emily's lap as a pillow, almost falling asleep.

"Hm?" She looked up. It took a moment to recall what Emily had said. "I didn't, I was watching a marathon of some home renovation show with Maryanne." It was hard to pay attention with those long, clever fingers running through her hair.

"On the news last night they were saying that the serial killer in Toronto was actually a necromancer."

Cora tensed. "Ah..." She'd known, of course. All reapers had known, because it was up to them to deal with it. Calling it a serial killer just made it easier to control panic, so people didn't freak out over someone trying to raise the dead. While the idea was scary, there were many reasons not to panic. The most important being: "It's impossible to bring back the dead. Once every few decades someone tries, but they never succeed." And it always ended in tragedy.

Emily considered that for a moment, her hand going still. "Is it odd to find that reassuring?"

"Not when you watch as many scary movies as you do," she teased, hoping to keep things light. It was odd that the truth had come out on the news, since the news should have spread among the reapers before then. If only to make damage control easier. Of course, social media and the internet being what it was, perhaps it shouldn't have been such a surprise, even if one of her brother's friends had been assigned to deal with the rogue reaper.

Emily grinned, fingers moving through Cora's hair again. "I guess I can understand the temptation, especially when you're dealing with death all the time."

"Yeah..."

"What happens to the necromancer? They didn't say, just announced that the deaths had stopped. I guess they assumed the necromancer had been stopped?"

She took a deep breath. "It always ends in death. Because they won't stop, not until someone forces them to. The lengths they go to... they spend too much time on the other side of the Veil, and it warps their mind." Of course, everything she knew was what had been told through stories and histories. Her parents had been very young when the last reaper had gone rogue.

"Oh..."

"Yeah... it's... it's not pleasant for anyone involved." She would have to ask her brother, Jet, if he knew anything the next time she spoke to him. The fallout would inevitably be a nightmare.

"It doesn't sound like it." Emily sipped her wine. "What do you want to watch tonight? Zombies? A romantic comedy? Dust motes floating through the air?"

Cora snorted, grateful for the change in conversation. Still, the topic had sapped some of the good mood she'd managed to regain. "I dunno."

Emily looked down, examining Cora's expression and thinking for a moment. "There is another option," she said at last. "We could go up to your room, break out that lovely bottle of massage oil you like, and I can make you feel really good before you fall asleep."

Just like that her mind was made up. "That sounds like the best idea I've heard all day," she replied, quickly finishing her wine.

Emily did the same. "I'm known to have them once in a while." When Cora sat up, Emily stood and took her hand, gently pulling her upright and leading the way up to her bedroom. It wasn't long before thoughts of necromancers and insecurities were pushed far from Cora's mind as Emily's clever hands made good on her promise.

2

It was very early in the morning when Cora's phone rang, dragging her out of a deep sleep. She glared at the glowing screen, but when she saw the number she answered right away. The Royal Newfoundland Constabulary didn't exactly do social calls.

"Cora? This is Detective Mike Byrne." There was something odd about his tone that had her sitting up, fully awake.

"What's wrong?" She felt Emily shifting beside her as she woke up and turned on the bedside light.

"I'm sorry, but I need you to meet me at the harbour as soon as possible." He took an audible breath and let it out slowly. "Its better if I explain once you're here."

"Of course. I'll be there soon." She trusted that Mike wouldn't waste her time. She'd worked with him a few times since moving back, and her brother had worked with him before that.

"Thanks." He hung up.

"What happened?" Emily wondered as Cora stretched and got out of bed, muscles still wonderfully loose from the massage.

"Detective Byrne called, so I can only assume that at least one person is dead." Sometimes reapers could help, if the soul still lingered, or if there was something urgent that required their soul to be found. But they weren't infallible.

"Ah."

"Yeah..." she ran a hand through her hair in an effort to get it into some kind of order before giving up and pulling it into a quick ponytail. She was grateful that it had grown long enough to do that again. "You should go back to sleep. I probably won't be home by the time you leave for work." She hauled on whatever she could find for clothes. Fashion wasn't a major concern at four-thirty in the morning. "Maryanne will cook you something for breakfast, I'm sure."

Emily sat up, letting the blankets pool around her waist as she pulled Cora in for a kiss. "Go be a superhero and solve crime, don't worry about me. Will I see you tonight?"

"I hope so." She managed a slight grin. "Jet, Lily, and I are having supper with Dad, but after that I'm free." Her mother was in Japan for another month doing research and training. Like Cora and Jet, she was a reaper, while Cora's father and sister were human, although Lily was a clairvoyant. While it was a coin toss if a reaper's children would be reapers, they were all touched by the powers beyond the Veil. Her father was a professor of folklore at the Memorial University of Newfoundland while Lily worked for the reapers in records and archives.

"Is Jet going to announce his engagement yet?"

Cora snorted as she shrugged into a sweater. It probably wasn't going to be warm enough, but she didn't really care. "He'll probably announce that he *thinks* he found the perfect ring and change his mind when he goes to buy it. I don't know why he's so nervous. Christine is going to say yes." Her brother had gotten lucky, finding someone who completely accepted him.

"I can't wait to hear about it." Emily kissed her again before letting her go and lying down again. Cora turned off the light and headed to the office. Maryanne didn't sleep, so at night she tended to be on the computer or in the space she'd created for herself in the attic.

Luckily, she caught Maryanne as she drifted through the door. "What happened? You're not usually up this early."

"Mike called, needs me at the harbour now."

She frowned. "That can't be good. Go on, I'll make sure Emily has a good breakfast, and that there's something for you when you get back."

"Thanks." She hurried out the door, barely remembering to grab her purse and keys. Her knife was already strapped to her thigh. Thinking back on the call, something in Mike's tone bothered her. He'd been on the force for over a decade, though she wasn't sure exactly how long. He'd only been in town a few years and had worked in central Newfoundland before that. Still, he'd dealt with his fair share of bodies, enough to be able to separate himself from it. But on the call he'd sounded shaken.

She drove a little faster, pushing the speed limit as she drove through the nearly empty streets.

When she made it to the harbour, the guard waved her through as soon as he saw her eyes. The fear she saw in his own eyes put her on edge. She parked by the detective's car, making sure that she had an easy path out again, just in case. While she trusted Mike, the others at the scene might not take so kindly to her presence, especially if her suspicions were right. The floodlights set up were not a promising sign, nor was the heavy equipment lined up along the dock, the kind that looked like it was meant to pull a boat out of the water.

"Morrigan," Mike said by way of greeting when he saw her. He was the type to address people by their last name in a work setting. A little taller than her, with a stocky build and a receding hairline, Detective Mike Byrne was an authoritative figure.

"Byrne," she mimicked out of habit as she looked around at the scene. There was a lot of activity, but not a lot of talking, and the unease in the air made her skin prickle. "What's going on?" She didn't bother with small talk, her stomach twisting in knots. The closer her fears came to being reality, the more she didn't want to deal with it. It wasn't going to be some grand adventure that made normal people kinder to her kin. She wouldn't be a hero at the end. No one would be. It would just be messy and awful for everyone involved.

He ran a hand through his thinning hair and let out a slow breath. "I don't know if its better to try to explain things or just show you first and go from there."

She grimaced. "Just show me."

He nodded and started walking over. "It's the second body we've found like it, which is why we called you in. The first was four days ago. We kept it quiet for the most part... but after the news last night..."

"Oh fuck." Even worse that she'd thought. Once they broke through the crowd, her stomach dropped as her suspicions were confirmed. The body was placed neatly in a dory that had the seats removed. It was painted a dusty purple and black combination that looked familiar, though out of place on a boat. The victim was male and naked, with arcane-looking symbols carved into his skin in strange patterns, concentrating around the heart and spiralling outward across his skin. "I'm guessing there's more on his back?"

Mike nodded. "They were on the last victim. We haven't turned him over fully to check yet. Do you know what any of the marks mean? We thought it might be someone high on something before, but this..."

"It's a necromancer," she said. From his expression, she was confirming his suspicion. The symbols looked like what she'd seen in the emails that had gone out a few weeks ago when they realized what they were dealing with in Toronto.

"What do the symbols mean?" Mike asked again as she walked around the body. The dory had been taken out of the water, likely around the same time Mike had called her.

"In the grand scheme of things? Nothing. Think of it like any of the movies where reading a creepy book makes things come back to life. Pick any ancient language. It'll likely be a combination of a few of them. The words might make sense, there might even be sensible phrases. But they won't *do* anything." She looked around. "The dead *cannot* be brought back to life. It's impossible." She added for emphasis, making sure her voice carried. Imaginations had a tendency to run wild in these situations, and she dreaded the thought of anyone finding out that the necromancer was not only still active, but in St John's. The term 'witch hunt' came to mind, with her burning at the stake.

"Don't worry, everyone here should know better than to believe scary stories," Mike added at a similar volume. "And with last night's news, we'll be *very* careful to keep this under wraps." Even though she could see a few reporters outside the gates, trying to get a shot or to get someone's attention for an interview.

Cora knelt to get a better look at both the body and the boat while she pulled out her phone to compare the photos she had with the current victim, looking for how things had changed since the necromancer had moved locations, and taking notes. Those would go to Cyrus Viduus, the current investigator, as well as the head of her own family, since the necromancer was now in a territory that fell under their the responsibility of the Morrigan line.

"How can we be certain this necromancer will act the same as the last?" Mike wondered, watching her and directing the people around them at the same time.

"Well, they won't. The last necromancer was in the sixties and science and technology have come a long way since then. You couldn't just search for dead languages or ways to preserve a corpse online like you can now."

"What?" Mike seemed oddly confused when she looked up from her notes.

"What?" His confusion was confusing to her.

"Are you saying this is the necromancer from Toronto?"

"Yes."

"How can you be sure?"

Admittedly that was a fair question. "There's never more than one in a generation, because that serves as a warning for everyone. There aren't that many reapers, not compared to how many mediums or clairvoyants. Add in regular humans and the numbers looked even smaller. This is going to affect all of us for a long time and in many unpleasant ways." She stood, not making eye contact with any of the others. "People are going to be more afraid of us than ever, and fear makes people do cruel things."

"If there are so few of you, how do you not know who it is?" The question came from one of the techs.

"Because they hide it. They know what they're doing is wrong and they do the best they can to hide it, especially in the early stages when there aren't any physical symptoms." She sighed. "Right now, there are people in every family looking through the last five years of records for anyone on active duty, and then they'll go through records of those who are inactive, and finally those who never became active. Anyone who looks the least bit suspect will be called in for a full evaluation." She looked around them. "The world might seem smaller, but its also much bigger, and many of us are constantly moving around, especially in the larger families. It's hard to keep track of everyone at once." It didn't help that the world seemed to be going to hell. Reapers could spend just days or maybe months in any given country, let alone a city, before jumping to the next place they were needed. She'd spent a few years like that.

"Okay..." Mike sighed and ran a hand through his hair. "This is going to be fun."

"For your purposes treat this like a serial killer, but don't approach anyone without our investigator," she instructed. "It will be too dangerous for your people."

"I will have to arrest them," he pointed out.

She shook her head. "There's only one way to stop a necromancer, Detective. Death. Your department should have some files relating to that, and I'll have more information sent to you."

He narrowed his eyes at her. "That's murder."

She didn't flinch, didn't back down, but the censure hurt, even though it would most likely be Cyrus killing the necromancer. "I know, but they won't stop,they can't, and there is no other way to stop them. If you put them in prison they'll escape through a tear. If you chain them in place they'll fill their cell with poltergeists. There's no way to cure the madness that consumes them and no way to heal the damage they end up doing to themselves." It would eventually kill them, a slow and painful death.

"It's still murder."

"I never said it wasn't. But if you look at the last case, you'll find that the government accepted this a very long time ago." While she didn't exactly think of Mike as a friend, she did like working with him, and hoped this wouldn't ruin things between them. He wasn't like most of the other detectives she'd worked with. He treated her like a regular person. Mike pressed his lips into a thin line but said nothing more about it. She turned her attention back to the boat, to the colours of it, and went back to the case notes in her email. Something was trying to add up in her mind, but it took a moment. "Hang on... isn't there a house these colours by the basilica?"

Silence fell for a moment, before the photographer spoke up. "Yeah, its pretty much across the street," she said, taking a closer picture of the paint.

Mike frowned. "Could that be relevant?"

"Around Toronto the bodies were found in painted boxes, but there didn't seem to be a rhyme or reason to the colours, at least, not one Cyrus could find. Some were similar, some were different. All that was the same was the size of the box."

"Serial killers tend to be creatures of habit."

She nodded. "One difference for necromancers is that they will make adjustments and changes over time as they try to find the right combination of things to bring back the dead." She flicked back through the email. "The actual murder sites were never found."

Mike looked over her shoulder and she pulled up pictures of the boxes so he could see. "What if they were giving away the scene of the crime?" He was reaching the same conclusion she was. "But that brings up more questions, like why they would do that and why change from boxes to dories?"

"The change could be because of the area, or something to do with salt water. There are tons of myths and stories in folklore surrounding salt water. But I think it would be a good idea to check the house."

"I need something more solid than that to get a search warrant."

"It'll take ages to find the right houses in Toronto. There's not a lot of colour variation like there is here." She tried to think. "A necromancer in the city isn't enough?"

"Could we contact or track down John Doe's ghost?"

She shook her head. "Its trapped. Like someone put it in that ghost cell you guys have." Which had been built the first time she'd worked with the detective. That had been a hell of a case.

"How can you tell?"

She blinked at him. "Because I'm a reaper?"

That earned her a cross between a raised brow and a grimace. "I should have seen that coming."

She shrugged apologetically. That was the best way to explain it, her ability to sense the lingering connection between the soul and the body. She could tell if the soul had moved on, if it lingered, or if it was trapped. "What if we can connect the first body to a house as well? If we can show a pattern, that should be enough."

Mike sighed. "Fine. I'll see what I can do. But you're coming with me when I go ask for it. And I'll look into the other body."

She nodded, half-expecting that deal was coming. They went over the site a few more times and then Mike drove her to the site where the first body had been found, nearer to the mouth of the harbour. She took more pictures and made sure to take notes of anything that would be needed in the reports while mentally going through everything that had to get done right away. At the top of the list was calling her brother so she could find out how to contact Cyrus. Then they would both have to contact the respective heads of their families to find out if Cyrus would continue to be the only investigator or if someone from Cora's family would step in.

"I'll look into houses as well, see if I can track down connections of some kind," she said as they returned to the second murder site, tapping her fingers against the car door as she thought. She could feel a headache coming on and it was only just after sunrise.

"Go home, I'll send you what we have on the last body and if you decide you want to have a look for yourself, it hasn't been released to the family yet."

"Okay. I'll send you the information on necromancers and anything else I can find." She got out of Mike's car and headed to her own, able to feel the eyes of the RNC people on her as she drove off.

As she'd predicted, Emily was gone by the time she got home. Cora just wanted to flop down on the couch, but she couldn't. There was a necromancer at large.

"How bad is it?" Maryanne asked as she floated into the room.

"The necromancer is here," Cora replied, trying to run a hand through her hair and forgetting it was in a ponytail.

"Well... that's about as bad as it can get, isn't it?" Maryanne asked.

"Pretty much. And there's already two bodies here on top of who knows how many in Ontario." From the last report she'd seen, Cyrus had been fairly certain that not all of the victims had been found.

"Do you think the necromancer will move again?"

Cora grimaced. She really hadn't needed that thought. "I hope not. I mean, we have the Queen's Road tear, so I kind of doubt it." It was one of the reasons her family was in St John's specifically. The tear was in an old house on Queens Road. They weren't quite sure how long it had been there, just that nothing they'd tried would close it. Every generation kept trying and worked to keep too many ghosts from coming back through it. Still, the house was one of the most haunted in the city. Currently, it was Jet's responsibility.

"Right. If there's anything I can do to help, let me know."

"Maybe, but we have to identify the murder scene first. And right now, I have to call Jet and get Cyrus's number." Jet would need to know anyway since he was technically in charge of the province while their mother was away. "And call Mom. And make a list of everything I need to do in the next hour."

"Go do that, I'll bring up some breakfast for you," Maryanne ordered. Cora nodded and went upstairs, allowing herself to take a deep breath before calling Jet and turning on her computer to send the files to Mike.

"What's wrong?" Her brother sounded half asleep. Which was fair considering it was still only half past seven in the morning.

She didn't waste time. "The necromancer moved here."

"What?"

"The necromancer is in St John's." She gave him a fast rundown of what she'd found at the crime scene. "I need Cyrus's number." She looked over as Maryanne entered and quietly left a plate of food on the desk, floating down through the floor as Cora nodded her thanks.

"Shit." She heard the muffled sounds of her brother getting up and speaking to someone else, most likely his girlfriend. "You know, I haven't heard from Cyrus in a while, but this is a pretty urgent case." There was a pause before he recited the number. "Call him now, I don't think he'll give a shit that it's four in the morning there and call me back after. Want me to call Mom?"

"Yeah, I have to call Lady Morrigan... should I call the Viduus family head too?"

There was another pause. "Talk to Cyrus first, and if you leave a message give him a few hours to reply. It's better if you call with more information than less. Did you send Mike the files he needs?"

"Sending as we speak."

"Alright. For the houses, you could talk to Alan. He might have an easier time getting records because he's at the university library."

"He's back from Edmonton?" Alan Dearil was a reaper from Alberta who'd moved to town a few months ago to attend Memorial University for a master's degree. He'd mentioned what he was studying, but Cora couldn't remember what it was. Possibly folklore or history? Maybe both? Either way, she didn't see much of him, since he was usually working, researching, or travelling.

"I think he was supposed to get back yesterday. I ran into him before he left. D'you have his number?"

"I'm pretty sure..." she looked through her contacts. "Yeah, I got it."

"Okay, let me know how it goes, and tell him to call me when he can."

"Will do." After a quick goodbye, she hung up and made a list of what she needed to do. As she was dialling Cyrus's number, she got a reply from Mike that he'd received her email and included the files she'd needed from him. She started looking through them as the phone rang. And kept ringing. Sighing as the voicemail kicked in, she left a quick, urgent message before hanging up and following that with a text, just in case. Cora tried not to read into it as she ate quickly and braced herself for the call with Lady Morrigan. She'd met the formidable old woman two or three times, and it never got easier. If rumours were true, most of the European family heads felt similarly.

It wasn't so much a force of power, but of personality. The head of the family had to deal with diplomacy issues, heads of state that didn't understand or didn't care about what a reaper's role in the world was. Sometimes the role was easier, sometimes it was hard. She thought of the German reapers during World War II, or really anyone in a conflict zone. She'd been to some of them during her years of travelling, but that felt different. She belonged somewhere else and could pack up and leave when she wanted. The others couldn't. Someone had to care for the dead who couldn't, or wouldn't, move on.

Maybe she'd get lucky and Cyrus would call back and deal with everything. In the meantime, she got up and sent Alan a text asking when he'd be at work before getting a shower.

She had a feeling her long day wasn't nearly over.

3

Two hours later she was walking into the MUN library and heading to the archives. She'd been there often for information on cases. One of the upsides was that no one asked why she wore sunglasses inside, either it wasn't remarkable enough on a university campus or they were too busy studying. It might have even been possible to get away with skipping them entirely, but she wasn't quite up for that.

Alan waved at her from the desk. Unlike her, her wore coloured contacts to hide that he was a reaper. She didn't like hiding who she was, and it felt like a step too far. He was a head taller than her, with messy blond hair and skin even paler than her own.

"Hey, how was your trip?" She asked when she headed over to him.

"Good, nice to see family once in a while" he replied. "What can I help you with?"

"I need help with property histories."

"Oh? Looking to buy a house?"

"I did that, it was haunted anyway. Is there somewhere private we can talk?" She couldn't talk about the investigation, let alone the necromancer, out here in the open.

He frowned, but nodded, waving for her to follow him. They ended up in a broom cupboard of an office. "Midterms are coming up, so all the study rooms are taken," he apologized, shutting the door behind them.

"It's fine," Cora assured him, then gave him a similar summary she'd given Jet, though she kept it more vague.

Alan's eyes were wide by the end. "That's a hell of a discovery," he said, rubbing the back of his neck. "Have you told Cyrus yet? He's the case lead, isn't he?"

"He's the lead, and I'm waiting for him to call me back," she replied.

"Alright. I'll send what I find to you in the meantime. Got any addresses for me to start with?"

Cora nodded and wrote the two addresses they suspected on paper, along with the colours of the houses. "Start with these two."

"Am I looking for anything in particular or just general?"

"Stay general, but we are looking for an excuse to search the houses to confirm they were the murder sites." She gave him a wry look. "For some reason people don't tend to respond well when you knock on their doors and ask them to see if someone committed a murder in their house." She'd probably try just asking the homeowners anyway, but experience taught her that rarely went well.

"That is true."

"You were active once, weren't you?"

He grimaced. "I was, but research is more my thing. I want to help out, but... dealing with souls isn't easy."

"No, its not," she agreed.

"I'll see what I can find."

"Thanks, I know you must be busy."

He shrugged. "I'm sure I can find a way to work property history into my thesis. Once I check these out I'll start looking and see if there's anything more, but I don't think a pattern will show until there's another body."

Now Cora grimaced. She seemed to be doing that a lot lately. "I didn't want to hear that." Her phone buzzed, but a quick glance showed that it wasn't Cyrus calling her back, so she put it back in her pocket.

"Sorry to be the bearer of bad news." He opened the door again to let her out.

"I'll try to keep you up to date," she promised, waving as she headed out. He waved back and returned to the front desk. At her car, she pulled out her phone to answer Emily's text.

<How are things going?>

Cora bit down on her lower lip, trying to figure out how to respond. <Not great>

<Anything you can talk about?>

<Not really, sorry>

<Okay. Good luck! Enjoy dinner with your family>

Part of her wished she could tell Emily everything, but part of her was glad she couldn't. Would this be the line? The one where being with her became 'too much.' The knowledge that reapers sometimes went crazy and tried to bring back the dead hadn't done it... yet. But getting close to the investigation... that might be the one.

<Thanks>

Cora went home after that and collapsed onto the couch. Somehow, it was only morning and she couldn't wait to go to sleep. Instead she had to figure out what to do now. She tried calling Cyrus again, and left another message. It was hard to sit still knowing what was going on, but she didn't know how much more she could do right now.

"Hear anything yet?" Maryanne wondered, drifting into the room.

"Nope." She covered her eyes with her forearm. "I'll give him another few hours, then I'm calling Lord

Viduus and Lady Morrigan." She grimaced, hoping it wouldn't come to that.

"Alright. How about you take some painkillers and we watch something while you wait? One of the Halloween baking shows should be starting in a few minutes."

Cora dragged herself upright to make room for Maryanne. "Sounds good."

Three hours later, there was still nothing. So Cora looked up the contact information for Lord Viduus's office. Predictably, as soon as she gave her reason for calling, she was put through to Lord Viduus himself.

"Caio, Signorina Morrigan. What can I help you with?" Lor Viduus was fairly new to the role, if Cora remembered correctly. The selection process varied between families and was a closely guarded secret.

"I'm sorry for disturbing you, Lord Viduus, so I'll get to the point." She had no idea what time it was in Italy. "The necromancer moved from Toronto, Ontario to St John's, Newfoundland. I've been trying to contact Cyrus since early this morning but haven't received a reply. Two bodies have already been found."

Lord Viduus was silent for a long moment before replying. "We've been keeping it quiet, but the truth is that we haven't heard from Cyrus in two weeks. That was his last report, and he's supposed to report in every three days."

"Two weeks?" That... there was no way that was good.

"Si. We have found no activity, either on our own network or through other channels. The announcement by the Canadian police made us hopeful that he would resurface, but it seems he is still missing."

Cora had no idea what to say.

"The most important thing now is to stop the necromancer. I will hand the investigation to your family until he is found." But there was a dark undertone to the other reaper's voice that she tried not to read into. "I will contact Lady Morrigan shortly, and I advise you to do the same."

"Yes."

Lord Viduus sighed. "We'll turn our resources to finding Cyrus. Any assistance you require is yours." He seemed to assume that *she* would be the one taking over the investigation.

"Thank you." They said their goodbyes and ended the call. Cora put her phone down and took a shaky breath. She didn't want this to happen. As selfish as it was, her life was finally looking good and she didn't to screw it up. She was used to murder mysteries, but this was a fucking horror story and it was starting to look like she was in the middle of it.

She dialled the number for Lady Morrigan but didn't press call. Instead she backed out and called her brother first.

"What's new?"

"Jet... Cyrus hasn't reported in for over two weeks." There was a long pause. "I'm sorry."

"Fuck..." There was another long pause. "Okay... so they'll need someone to take over, right?" She could always count on him to keep his head in a crisis.

"At least until he contacts someone." She didn't want to say he was missing, that made it too real.

"Right." There was a pause, like he was trying to decide to say something, so she waited. "You realize Lady Morrigan will probably ask you to take the case, right?" As the first on the scene and was currently doing the investigations, she was the likely candidate to take over. Even though she was the youngest reaper in the province, she was twenty-six. She wasn't a child anymore.

"Well, it has to be dealt with, doesn't it?"

"Yeah, but if you don't want to handle it, or you don't think you can, we can ask Mom to come back and I'll take it."

She considered his offer for a moment. "Do you think I can do it?" It shouldn't have mattered, but she'd always looked up to her brother.

"Killing isn't what we do," he pointed out. "Its not a question of what you're capable of. If you had to find and kill the necromancer, you would. I don't doubt that. But if you don't want to do it, there are other options. Whatever you choose, I'm here and I'll do whatever I can to help you."

"Thanks," was all she could say, and she meant it.

"Let me know as soon as you find out."

"I'll call as soon as I hang up."

"Good." She ended the call and took one more deep breath before dialling Lady Morrigan's number with shaking fingers. This was not how she'd imagined today going. Once again, a quick explanation had her put straight through to the matriarch of her entire family.

"This is Lady Morrigan." The elderly voice was unmistakably Irisht.

"Hi... this is Cora Morrigan, from Newfoundland, Canada."

"So, the necromancer is in your neck of the woods now." She must have spoken to Lord Viduus already.

"Yes, I tried to contact the current investigator, but have not received a reply. Have you spoken with Lord Viduus?"

"I have." There was a pause and Cora could hear typing. "You have been working closely with the local detectives, correct?"

"Yes."

Another pause. "And your brother worked closely with Cyrus until he took over duties from your mother?"

"Yes, they're still close."

"In that case, he's too close for this investigation. I want you to answer me honestly now, Cora. Are you able to handle this investigation? You have been cleared of suspicion."

Cora swallowed hard, hoping Lady Morrigan wouldn't hear that. "I can."

"Then I'm handing this investigation to you. I expect reports weekly and updates at least every three days. Call me directly." Cora grabbed paper and a pen as the head of her family rattled off her cell number. "I don't care what time it is."

"Yes."

"Be careful and good luck. I will tell Viduus to release the full case file to you."

"Thank you."

"Don't thank me, Cora. Not for this. If you have any doubts or run into *any* trouble, call. Whatever resources you need will be at your disposal."

"Yes, Lady Morrigan."

"Then goodbye, I will ensure you get the files."

"Goodbye." She ended the call, and immediately called her brother back.

He answered straightaway. "Well?"

"I'm on the case. Lady Morrigan thought you might be too close to it all with Cyrus missing."

"Yeah, I can see that. Anything you want, I'm here."

"Alright. I'm going to get started, I guess. You still going to Dad's for dinner?"

"Yeah, before you start you should call Mom, though."

"Right." That was going to be a fun conversation.

"Are you going to tell Emily?"

"I... I don't know. Should I?" She didn't want to.

"Maybe? I mean, this is going to take up most of your life and she'll probably find out sooner or later."

"Right..." She would rather tell her mother she was going to be hunting down a necromancer.

"Think about it, anyway. And let me know if you hear anything about Cyrus."

"I will." She hung up and put her head on her desk.

Five days later, Cora had made little progress. It was both frustrating and expected. In the meantime, two more bodies were found, two days apart. Despite the extra surveillance on the harbour, both bodies were left there, neatly placed in brightly coloured dories, and no one could figure out how it was happening. They were able to match the boats to two more houses, so at least a pattern was emerging. Now they just had to make sense of it and follow it back to its creator. One upside was that Mike managed to get his hands on an open search warrant for any properties they thought might be connected to the necromancer.

Which would have been great, if there had been any evidence to find. So far, each site had been meticulously cleaned, not even a fingerprint or drop of blood left. There was no sign of forced entry, nothing from the neighbours about seeing someone who shouldn't have been there. The fact that they couldn't tell anyone exactly why they were searching didn't help either, and Cora's presence seemed to make things worse.

"I'd say not to take it personally, but that'd be pretty useless, wouldn't it?" Mike said as they walked from his car to the house. Her vehicle was back at the RNC headquarters. The last homeowners had been particularly cold toward her.

Cora pushed her sunglasses up on her nose. "Pretty much." She looked around at the Halloween decorations on the houses. The big night was a week away, when the Veil would be at its thinnest and ghosts would be able to communicate with the living without having to cross the threshold and wihtout a medium or clairvoyant. Tears acted like beacons on Halloween, so Jet was getting ready for a long, sleepless night, and so was she. Even though the necromancer took precedence, the tear on

Queen's Road was far too active on a normal night for one person to handle Halloween alone. She really hoped she'd have the case closed by then, but she knew it was about as likely as winning the lottery without buying a ticket.

"Did you go out for candy as a kid?" Mike wondered, pulling her mind back to the present.

"Yeah," she smiled slightly. "Dad would take the three of us out while Mom worked." One of their cousins would usually fly in to help her. "When we got older we'd help her."

"Ah. So, what's your bet for the alibi: closing up the cabin, on a tropical cruise, or on the mainland? This house is owned by an older couple."

She considered. "I'd say cabin. It's that time of year." That was part of the pattern: no one was home at the time, usually for a few days. Enough time to set up, commit both the murder and the ritual, and then clean up and leave. There was enough to show that *something* had been there, that *someone* had been there, but that was it. The basements were left too clean, with things out of place, but there was no DNA, no fingerprints, nothing. It was like the necromancer was a ghost.

Mike knocked on the door and did the introductions and vague explanations, the assurances that the homeowners weren't suspects. Nothing seemed to rattle him. Ever. It wasn't long before they were walking into the house while the homeowners talked. They'd been closing up a cabin near Carbonear. No one had called to tell them that anything was amiss. But when they'd returned home, they had noticed the basement was cleaner than they'd left it, some things moved around, though nothing was missing. They'd just thought one of them had cleaned it and forgotten to mention it. Cora followed Mike down to the basement while the rest of the team did their more meticulous work. Once there she took off her sunglasses while they looked around. There was no ghost, no residual energy from a tear being opened, but that would have dissipated after a few hours anyway.

"See anything?" She had a little training in forensics, enough for her normal work, but not nearly enough to thoroughly examine a crime scene.

"Not really," Mike replied. "Just that it's as spotless as the other three. And while we can call that evidence, its not the kind of evidence we *need*." He sighed and ran a hand through his thinning hair. "How are... these people usually caught?" He knew better than to say 'necromancer' where people not involved in the investigation could hear. People around here tended to gossip, and secrets rarely stayed that way for long.

"They make a mistake; they go after one of their own and the fight attracts attention. Luck. The background checks usually narrow it down enough to make it easier, but that's gotten harder as the world's gotten bigger and moving around is easier." She'd read more on necromancers in the past week than she'd ever wanted to know.

"Did your contact find any pattern in the houses that our guys missed?" Because they hadn't found anything worth noting.

"Maybe. I was talking to him yesterday and he thought he might be onto something. Have you found any connection between the victims and the houses?"

"Nothing recorded, and I have to wait until we can release the victims' names before I can check on connections between them and the homeowners."

"Why the wait?"

"We're working on framing this as a serial killer, and given how few people are in on it, its a bit more work than usual." He sighed. "People are still gonna talk, especially since Toronto is still making headlines, but we can try to control things. There's also a possibility that our friend got the information about the houses being empty from social media sites. They aren't that hard to hack. There's also bank records, phones, and everything else. Hell, they could've heard through the grapevine." He sighed again and got the rest of the crew down to do their futile sweep.

"I still don't understand how they can get from the house to the harbour with a boat and a body and not get caught at any point," Mike muttered once they were back in his car. Cora felt like shit. People were dying and she was doing so little about it. She couldn't do much more, but it still felt like she *should* be doing more.

"The neighbours might not have seen them, but there might be a ghost or two that did," she suggested, watching one cross the street out of the corner of her eye. "Most of the ghosts around here are connected to the properties they're on, but some might have more portable anchors." Like Maryanne, her spirit tied to a ring. If they could move their anchor with telekinetic powers, they could potentially cover a large distance. Though her understanding was that anchors took more energy to move than most other objects. Which was why Maryanne didn't just head to the paint store on her own whenever she wanted to redecorate. "I can try to talk to them."

"Why didn't you think of that sooner?" Mike wondered.

"Because its rarely useful. Unless they happened to be in the right place at the right time, they wouldn't have seen anything. And aside from their tendency to run away from reapers, ghosts gossip even more than grandmothers do at bingo."

"Fair enough. How will you get them to talk to you, then?"

"I'll take my housemate with me. She'll approach them first and try to convince them it's safe."

"The ghost?"

"Yeah." Mike had met Maryanne on a few occasions.

"Alright." He paused for a second as he moved to start the car, and she waited for him to say whatever was on his mind. "Have you talked to your buddy? The one who was after the necromancer before you?"

"Cyrus? No, I haven't." It was a growing source of worry. The reaper seemed to have vanished into thin air. Jet was especially worried about the situation.

"Have you ever considered that he might be the necromancer?"

"He would have been cleared before he took the case."

"But people can make mistakes. And he's been missing for a while. Besides, being involved would be one of the best cover-ups." He held up his hands before she could say anything. "I know you've said he was your brother's friend, but what if he figured out that would make it easier to cover his tracks by coming here? It is one of the reasons why they wanted you on the case and not Jet, isn't it?"

The worst thing was, he had a point. "I'll look into it," she said reluctantly. Once a reaper crossed the line into necromancy... there was really no telling what they would do.

"I want to be wrong, but you have to stay open to all possibilities until they can be absolutely ruled out," he said, his tone not unkind as he started the car.

Cora pressed her lips together and nodded. "Me too." Mike pulled out of the parking spot and they were saved from an awkward silence when Cora's phone rang. "Its Alan," she said, pulling out her notebook and a pen before answering. Mike turned off the radio so she could hear better. "Hello?"

"Hey, I have something. It's small, but it might be useful." Alan sounded out of breath, and excited.

"I'll take anything."

"So, I checked the addresses against the reaper archives, including the last one you sent me, and I found something interesting. Most of the houses here, especially downtown, are really old, right?"

"Yes..."

"Well, a lot of them show up in the records, some more than once, as having ghosts, or some kind of death happened inside them. But the houses you sent me, they have nothing. I looked a little deeper, and there's no stories, no rumours, no mention of any ghosts in any of them. Kinda weird for houses that are over a hundred years old, eh?" He said all of that with barely a breath. "I mean, at least two of them have burnt down completely over the years, but still. And I'm sorry, I've been drinking way too much coffee and sleeping too little lately."

"That's fine, its not a fun time for anyone right now. But why go for houses like that in particular? Is having a... blank slate really that important?"

"Maybe? I mean, it could be that because no one died or died and crossed over there's no 'bad energy' or any of that stuff. It's a blank canvas, and that might make their chances of actually bringing someone back to life better. Besides, it'd be easy to find a house like that in some new suburb of Toronto, barring any First Nations burial sites. But this isn't a horror novel. Although that would be something else to look into."

"Right." She added that to her notes. "If nothing else we'll be able to eliminate some houses from the list of potential addresses in Toronto."

"Exactly. I'll call if I find anything else. I've got a mountain of grading to get through as well."

"Thanks, and don't forget to sleep. I have a feeling we'll all have some long nights coming up."

"Right."

"Thanks again."

"No problem." He hung up and Cora relayed the information to the detective.

"Interesting... well, it could help give us a list of places to keep an eye on."

"I guess so. Still, I'm going to see if I can talk to some of the local restless dead."

"Tonight?"

She shook her head. "I'm going to see if we have any files on the ghosts first, any information that might help when questioning them."

"Would a medium or clairvoyant be able to help?"

She considered. "Thanks, but its better if I do it. I'll start with the first house since our friend might not have been so careful the first time around."

"Good call."

She hoped so.

"Of course, I'll help," Maryanne said when Cora explained things. They were putting the Halloween decorations back up after shooting the Christmas photos that she needed. Even if Halloween had become more work than fun over a decade ago, Cora still enjoyed the aesthetic. She was a little bit of a goth, and didn't care if it played into stereotypes about reapers. "You know, this room would look lovely in a nice mint green."

Cora raised a brow. "You *just* repainted the house."

"No, I repainted the *inside* of the house. The house itself I was thinking ought to be more of a turquoise colour. Its been green long enough."

Cora though about that one. "If its the shade I'm thinking of I'll give you that one."

She clapped her hands, delighted. "I'll order the paint in the spring."

There was a knock on the door and Cora hopped off the chair she'd been standing on to go let Emily in. "Hey," she said, kissing her. She hadn't told Emily the truth about the investigation. Not yet. She wanted to. She knew Jet had been right, and both her parents had advised her to do the same in separate conversations. But whenever she tried to, her stomach tied itself in knots and it became hard to breathe.

"Hey," Emily said when she pulled away to breathe again. "How's the investigation going?"

Cora shrugged, the knots tying themselves up tight. "Not great, but I got some information that might help." She headed into the living room, Emily following.

"I see Christmas is over," she remarked.

"Just for now," Maryanne replied. "I'm not allowed to keep the decorations up until December." She looked at Cora, who raised a brow.

"We have a deal. Break it at your own risk," she reminded her housemate. "I *will* mix in the Halloween decorations."

Maryanne just shook her head and turned to Emily. "See what I have to deal with? Anyway, I'll have the photos ready to go online soon."

"Cool, I can't wait to see the album" She put her bag down by the couch. Cora tried to ignore the look that Maryanne gave her while Emily's back was to them. She knew her housemate also agreed with Jet. "So, what shall we do tonight?"

"Well, there's an amazing lasagna in the oven, so I figured we could eat that, and then we can see where the night takes us." She ran her fingers playfully over Emily's side. She needed to tell her the truth. It was allowed, possibly even necessary, because Emily could potentially become a target. It had happened before, a necromancer targeting the loved ones of the reaper heading the investigation. "Ah... actually... there's something I need to talk to you about." The knots in her stomach tightened and it felt like there was a vice around her chest, squeezing the air out of her lungs. Would this be it? Would this be the line? Jet's new fiancée was sticking beside him no matter what, but Stephanie was one in several million, and Jet wasn't hunting a creepy serial killer bent on trying to raise the dead. Even *thinking* that sounded crazy. Stephanie had also been with him for years, not months like her and Emily.

Emily frowned. "What's wrong?" Out of the corner of her eye, she saw Maryanne head upstairs, giving them some privacy. Cora gently tugged her to the couch and sat down, pulling her girlfriend down beside her.

"The investigation... it's not a normal murder case. The necromancer... they weren't stopped. They just moved here."

Her eyes went wide, and the knots in Cora's stomach became painfully tight. "Are you sure? How... how many have died?"

"I'm certain, and its four people here. We still don't know about the true total in Ontario. The... the reaper who was investigating went missing. So... I'm in charge of it now." It was hard to get a full breath in. Emily was very, very quiet for a long moment. Too long.

"Could you become a target? Why are you telling me if no one else knows?" Her kind had never been known for being open with information.

"I could become a target... and so could you." She swallowed hard and quickly continued. "There's only a small chance, but its happened in the past." Her lips felt numb as the words fell from them. "So, if you want-"

"Don't, Cora," Emily interrupted. "Don't suggest I leave you for this."

"Its just... I understand if its too much." Her voice was far weaker than she wanted it to sound.

"It's scary, but I'm not going to ditch you. Cora, I know enough about reapers to have some idea of what I'm getting into. I want to be with you, and some mad bastard isn't going to change that." She lightly caressed Cora's cheek. "I don't know what people have been like in your past, but I don't scare that easy." Cora started to speak, but Emily shook her head. "I know you won't believe me yet. We're still too new. But I'll prove it." She pulled Cora in and kissed her, long and slow. Cora sank into her, into the feeling of her lips. Emily was right. She wanted to believe her, she really did. But her heart had been broken often enough that she couldn't quite trust this. Emily slipped an arm around Cora's waist and tangled the fingers of her other hand in Cora's hair, while Cora gripped the back of her shirt, pulling her close. It was better to lose herself in this than the doubts. Better to have one more night while everything sank in and Emily realized what she was dealing with. Still, Cora hoped she was proven wrong. Even more, she hoped that the warning was entirely unnecessary. She'd rather have a broken heart than a dead lover. Only one of those could eventually be fixed.

4

The next evening, Cora and Maryanne got ready to talk to ghosts. The plan was to start in the Battery, at the site of the first murder. Then they would work their way through neighbourhoods in chronological order. It was the best idea she had.

Part of her felt guilty about putting it off for a night, but she had needed that time with Emily. She felt a bit more secure in their relationship, Emily knew what was going on, and most importantly, she hadn't run. It was a huge relief.

Less of a relief was the news she'd received about Cyrus that morning. The Viduus family had tasked mediums with locating Cyrus's soul in either plane of existence. It was the equivalent of deciding that they were looking for a body, and not a living person.

"Ready?" She asked Maryanne as she made sure her notebook was in her pocket.

"Yes." Maryanne handed over an old, battered morning ring. A lock of her hair was braided around a gold band. Her mother had it made after her death, and once her family realized she haunted it, they'd kept it safe, carefully preserving it until her several times great-niece died and it fell while her things were being cleared out of the house. She had no other living relatives.

"Let's go." Cora threaded a ribbon through the ring and tied it around her neck as they headed out. She left her sunglasses behind. The ghosts would know what she was and the living would avoid her.

It was late enough in the evening that there weren't many people around, though she also suspected that might be in part because rumours were starting to spread. The increased RNC and security presence around the harbour hadn't gone unnoticed, though Mike had assured her that no one was talking about the real reason they were there, and the bodies still hadn't been released to their families. She was sure they'd come up with some excuse to cover it up.

As it turned out, they didn't have to search too long before Maryanne found someone willing to talk. His name was Liam Walsh and it didn't surprise her when he stopped well out of reach while Maryanne moved to her side.

"You're here about them bodies, aren't you?" Liam asked, his voice heavily accented. "The ones they found in the harbour?" It didn't surprise her that he knew. He was old and powerful.

"That's right."

"If I answer 'em, will you try to take me?"

"Not at this moment," she hedged. "Solving this case is more important."

"Well, to start, I seen the bodies in the harbour, the ones the b'ys are hiding from everyone. I stays out where I can see it all."

"Okay, did you see who put them there?"

He shook his head. "Buddy was wearin' a... what d'you kids calls it? A hoodie. But I'm pretty sure he was male; he was doing some cursing. I couldn't see 'is face. I was too far away."

"Okay. And you're sure it was the same person?"

"Yeah, 'e went through them tears you send ghosts through. I didn't know living people could go through 'em too."

"Its not done often," she replied. It was both risky and unpleasant, and that was just for reapers.

"Anyway, Will saw 'im through the window once. Said there wasn't supposed to be anyone home for a few days yet."

"Have you checked the house to see if he's still there?" Cora wondered.

"I 'ave. There's no sign of 'im. I was wonderin' if one of you took 'im."

"I haven't, I'll look into it," she replied. "Anything else you want to add?"

"Nope, that's it."

"Okay." She let him go and looked at Maryanne. "Let's see if we can get anything more." She nodded, and they kept going around the neighbourhood. They didn't find anyone else who'd seen anything, though there were a few missing ghosts. The same happened around the other houses; ghosts who might have been in a position to see something were gone.

"They're all so frightened," Maryanne said as they left the last neighbourhood.

"I know." She sent her brother a message with a list of ghosts they should have been able to find.

"Do you think the missing ones are all trapped or killed?"

"I'm hoping not. If some of them were reaped we can get a medium to contact them. Unless he crossed over and killed them." But to do that he would have to physically walk through a tear instead of just sending his soul beyond the Veil. It was risky as hell and took far more energy. But for a necromancer, it would be part of their madness, breaking all the rules reapers held to. Spirits already beyond the Veil were meant to be left alone, to enjoy their afterlife.

"You can do that?"

"Yes, but its rare and its really risky." Because there was no guarantee that a soul could be caught before the reaper suffered permanent damage.

"Fair enough." Maryanne had seen her through recovery once before when she'd crossed for a case. Cora hated going over. It was cold, dark, and foggy to her eyes. So very cold.

"Not unless I absolutely have to." Her phone buzzed. "Can you check that?"

"Its Jet. He sent the grave locations and he hasn't reaped any of the ghosts," Maryanne read.

"Any popular cemeteries?"

"Four bodies are at Mount Carmel, including Liam's pal Will."

"Then we'll start there." As long as there was a fragment of bone, she could figure out where a soul was. That lingering connection, even through cremation, couldn't be broken by anything. It was also one of the reasons why spirits possessing people was the stuff of mythology and horror movies. Right now, she felt very lucky that none of the ghosts whose bodies had been cremated had also been scattered. She didn't want to have to contact the families to find out where they'd scattered the ashes so she could wander until she happened upon a fragment big enough.

This late at night the gates were locked, but she had keys for all of the cemeteries. Together with Maryanne, they scoured the graves until they found what they needed. Will had crossed, but the other three were either trapped or gone. Still, that was at least something.

"One out of four so far," she sighed. "And I'd say most likely the other three are dead."

"What if he realizes that Will is a loose end?"

Cora grimaced. "I hope not. We'll work fast, and he's got other things to focus on."

Maryanne nodded. "Well, now there's just the mystery of how he's getting around."

"Yeah... that one I can't explain. Did Liam say anything to you before you brought him to me?"

"I found him in a spot that overlooks the harbour, he said he was waiting for the silver light he saw ahead of the dories appearing."

That could only mean one thing. "Oh no..."

"What?"

"I think I know how the necromancer is getting past all the security, and into the houses without being seen." It was completely suicidal, but whoever it was would know that they had nothing left to lose.

"How?"

"He's using the tears. It's the stupidest thing imaginable, but you can use the Veil to travel, usually short distances. Anything long would be too draining. You make a tear, go through it, and once you're in, you can make another tear to go somewhere else. The longer the distance, the more it takes out of you."

"But I thought normal people died as soon as they crossed."

"Our magic can protect them for a short period of time." She grimaced. "I'll have to go through." Searching for random spirits would take time, which would mean she'd have a longer recovery period after. She'd have to make damn sure she found something good.

"Well then... you can't use a medium for that?"

"No, they need specific people to focus on. If they try something that broad they get overwhelmed. I have to go."

"Do you still want to check the other graveyards?"

"We might as well." Then she'd get ready.

Late that night she got a call from Alan, asking for her to see him at the university in the morning. He'd sounded excited. She got up early to go for a run first. With a career that often involved chasing ghosts, it was important to stay in shape. Especially when sometimes those ghosts used telekinesis to throw things at her. Not to mention the sheer insanity that was dealing with a poltergeist. Leaves crunched under her feet, hardened by the night's frost as she tried to clear her mind, to think of nothing at all and lose herself in the rhythm of running and the music playing in her ears. She tried not to focus on what she would be doing in a few very short hours.

It didn't work.

When she got home, she would call her brother and Mike Byrne, because she needed to be near a point the necromancer had already used. Time, space, and perception beyond the Veil played by different rules. Generally speaking, though, ghosts could be found in the same area time and time again, unless summoned elsewhere. There was a lot about that realm that she didn't know, and more that she wasn't allowed to know. Mike had assured her that they would be able to use the basement of the first house, and she didn't ask how he'd convinced the homeowners.

She tried to mentally prepare herself to spend the rest of the day, and possibly the next, trying to remember what it felt like to be warm. She didn't mind the cold, she lived in St John's for fuck's sake, where winter lasted half the year or more. But the literal soul-chilling space beyond the Veil was different. Ghosts didn't feel it, but living souls did. It was like kind of warning that they weren't supposed to be there.

Eventually she had to turn around and run home, still tense and keyed up. Maryanne already had a stack of pillows and blankets on the couch, ready for the aftermath. She was singing as she cleaned up, the song as familiar as it was eerie in her ghostly voice.

"Are you going to tell Emily?" She asked, hovering a few inches off the floor as she changed a bulb in one of the floor lamps.

Cora hadn't thought of that. "Ah..." She just kept walking to the stairs, hoping to get away without answering the question.

"I don't think she's going to run away scared if you tell her," Maryanne continued. "She hasn't so far."

"I know, but just because she likes watching horror movies doesn't mean she wants to be *in* one," Cora replied, using the bottom of her shirt to wipe sweat off her face.

"What are you going to tell her when she calls?"

Cora hadn't thought of that. "I don't know." She tapped her nails against the banister a few times and sighed. "Look, I'll tell her the truth if she calls, but I won't call her now. She'll just worry if she knows what I'm doing. That good enough?"

Maryanne raised a brow. "I don't know. Is it?"

"You sound like my mother," Cora grumbled as she headed upstairs.

"Technically I'm old enough to be your twice-great grandmother at least!" Maryanne replied, her tone bemused rather than offended. Cora rolled her eyes and headed up to the shower.

Alan was waiting for her behind the counter when she got to the library. "You feeling okay?" She asked. He looked pale and tired. But then, weren't they all?

"I'll sleep better once this case is solved," he replied, waiting for her to follow as he got out from behind the counter and waved for her to follow. They headed back into the cramped office. "How are you? You look like you could use more sleep too."

"I'll be fine," she replied. "What've you got for me?"

"So, I managed to set up an algorithm to compare the records of hauntings we have with current data, especially houses that have been destroyed and rebuilt or rebuilt using salvaged materials," he explained quickly. "Most of the houses or properties have been haunted at some point or other so I set up different lists for different factors that could affect how likely the necromancer is to see them as ideal spots."

Her eyes widened. "That's impressive. I didn't know you could do that."

He shrugged. "I study coding when I have spare time."

"Cool." He'd never mentioned it before.

"I'll call you later when the algorithm finishes running."

She started to nod, then stopped. "Actually, email or text would be better. I'm going to be out of commission for the rest of the day."

He frowned. "Oh? Why?"

"I'm going through the Veil. There are some ghosts I need to talk to."

"Wow... so it's come to that."

She grimaced. "Yeah."

"Do you need an anchor? I'd be happy to help."

"Thanks, but Jet's gonna do it." She managed a sheepish smile. "I'll feel more comfortable having my big brother there. But thanks for offering."

Alan nodded. "Good luck, I hope you find what you're looking for."

"Thanks," she said. "Anything else?"

"Yeah, actually... I looked into the list of people who'd accessed the records over the last month, and aside from myself or you and your brother, there's one more account that shows up more than once."

She frowned. "Who?"

"Cyrus Viduus."

Her brows went up. "When did he log in?" He'd been missing almost three weeks

"Latest was in the last few days."

Could he still be alive? Why hadn't he contacted anyone? "I'll let Lord Viduus know. He'll be able to get someone to track the IP address or network or something."

"I can do that," Alan offered. "You can focus on crossing the Veil."

She shook her head. "It'll just take a few minutes. Thanks for the info!" She turned to leave. Jet would be happy to know about Cyrus, unless... but no... Cyrus had to have been cleared before starting the investigation. But humans were fallible, mistakes could be made. She couldn't let herself think like that. It didn't do anyone any good.

She called Jet and Mike as she got in her car. Jet would meet her at her place since she wouldn't be able to drive herself home after crossing. With that arranged, she called Lord Viduus before driving home. He seemed grateful for the information, but also seemed to jump to the same conclusions she had. She wanted to be wrong. She wanted all of them to be wrong. But it wasn't looking good.

Her brother was already there when she got home. "Ready to do this?" He asked, leaning against his car.

She swallowed hard and nodded, waving to Maryanne when she saw her in the window. "Ready as I'll ever be." She got into his car when he unlocked her door. "Jet... there's something I need to tell you about Cyrus."

He looked over quickly as he shut the door and put his seatbelt on. "What happened?"

Cora explained what Alan had said about the database, trying as hard as she could to keep her suspicions from bleeding into her voice.

But her brother wasn't a fool. "You suspect him."

"I... I don't know. I mean, his login info could have been stolen as a way to throw us off the trail, but no one's seen or heard from him in weeks. I called Lord Viduus before I called you, and he's going to try tracking the IP address that used Cyrus's account."

"Right... but I don't think its him." Jet focused on the road as he started driving, though Cora wasn't sure he just didn't want to look at her.

"You don't *think* it's him or you don't *want* it to be him?" She couldn't help but turn Mike's question on him.

He glanced at her before turning his gaze back to the road. "Both." He took a deep breath and let it out slowly. "I kept in contact with him, even after I moved home to help Mom. I would have noticed if he started to go off the deep end."

"Everything says that the change is gradual," she reminded him. "Necromancers don't just wake up one day and decide to start playing Doctor Frankenstein." Maybe it was a little flippant, but she didn't try to take it back.

"I'm telling you, he doesn't have it in him," Jet insisted.

"Look, I don't *want* it to be him either, but right now all I have to go on is what I know. There's still every chance the ghosts can confirm that its not him."

"Right." They didn't speak much for the rest of the drive, and Mike was waiting for them at the door.

"Homeowners are both at work," he told them without preamble. If he noticed the tension between the siblings, he decided not to mention it. "They think we're doing another sweep of the crime scene. I figured it was better than going into detail."

"Good enough for me," Jet said, waving for Mike to precede them inside, as the detective was the one with a key.

"Will this be like last time?" Mike wondered as they stepped inside.

"Almost. I'll be gone longer though, and I have Jet."

"What difference does that make?"

"It's safer for me," she replied.

"Perfect," he said with a nod of approval. "Do you need me in the basement with you or stay up here?"

Last time she'd made him leave the room. There hadn't been time for explanations, and without an anchor, any distraction for her physical body could have caused her to lose focus and get lost beyond the Veil, which could be a fatal mistake. "Up to you. If you do stay, you'll have to do whatever Jet says and trust that he knows when I'm in trouble." While she would never go so far as to say that the detective had a hero complex, he did have a rather strong protective streak.

"You'll also have to have your phone and everything else on silent," Jet added. They all checked their phones then, and Jet and Cora turned theirs on silent.

"Then it's probably better that I stay upstairs," Mike said. "If something comes through I can't risk missing it, especially if its another body." They nodded and he headed back upstairs.

Jet looked at her. "Ready?"

She nodded and they sat on the floor facing each other. Cora pulled out her dagger and took a few deep breaths to relax as much as she could and to focus. Once she was ready, she drew a long, shallow cut along her forearm, focusing her power and creating a tear in her body. She put her dagger down as the cold started to seep into her body and reached out to her brother, ignoring the faint glow from the bleeding cut. Jet took both of her hands in his own, his skin warm against hers. Cora closed her eyes and focused again, drawing the magic that made her a reaper through her body, letting her soul slip through the tear she'd created. The blackness deepened as the warmth was leeched out of her, and when she opened her eyes she was surrounded by the dark, rolling fog beyond the Veil.

She knew this was just the way her living soul perceived the realm beyond the living, and that to the dead it would be something entirely different. What that was, she didn't know, and wouldn't until she died. The fog went in all directions, almost hiding the tear she'd made to get through. It was so very easy to get lost in this place, except that she could feel warmth from where her brother gripped the hands of her physical body. It served as a beacon, leading her back to herself. Trusting him not to let her go, she ventured forward. Talking to Will was a high priority, but he wouldn't be easy to find. So first she wandered, looking for anyone. Time and space played by different rules in this place, so she could be going thousands of kilometres or a few hundred meters.

"Hello? I need to talk to anyone who saw a reaper dragging the living through these lands." She had to tread carefully between specific and vague, enough to trigger a spirit's memories and have them answer her summons, but not so open that anyone would appear.

"I saw," a voice spoke. Cora turned to face the spirit that emerged from the fog, an older woman. "It was a cruel thing."

"What do you mean?"

"I might have died in Toronto, but my heart was always in Newfoundland, so I guess it was seen as fit for me to wander to where I would find my people after I died." She grinned slightly. "But don't ask about that, you're not allowed to know."

Cora was used to that kind of statement in this place. "Do you know who the necromancer is?" While it was entirely possible a spirit could lie, she doubted that would happen in this case.

The spirit shook her head. "Is that what he was? How dreadful. I never saw most of his face, only his eyes. The rest he kept covered." The old woman shivered, more of a leftover reflex than a physical response, since she didn't have those anymore. "He killed another like you here. But I suppose that's not very helpful, is it?"

Cora froze for a moment, staring at her before she could speak. "He killed Cyrus?"

"I don't know the name. But they both had eyes like yours. So, I guess they were both reapers."

She took a step back, going through the motions of taking a deep breath even though no air filled her lungs. "The... the body... what happened to it?" Did he take it or leave it to vanish in this place?

"Left where it fell, and it disappeared. Does that happen with everyone or just reapers?"

"Anything that doesn't belong here." No one quite knew what happened to it, another mystery the living were not allowed to have the answer to. But that wasn't important. What mattered was that she had to figure out how to tell Jet that his friend was not only innocent, but murdered. Hell, she would have to tell Cyrus's family. She'd never had to do that before. Everyone she'd had to deal with so far had already been dead, and known to be dead. What would she say?

"I'm so sorry, dear. Were you two close?"

She shook her head. "No. My brother was close to him."

"Ah, I'm sorry I couldn't be of more help."

Cora shook her head again. "No, even finding out this much is a huge help. We've been looking for him for weeks. Did... did the necromancer say anything?"

The woman paused, thinking. "He did, but his voice was too muffled to be able to tell you anything. He didn't seem happy about what he'd done. I'd say he even felt guilt. He didn't even notice me standing there."

"Good," Cora murmured, clenching hands into fists, though she couldn't feel the muscle tension without a body. "Thank you for your help."

"You're welcome. I hope you find the fucker." She laughed at Cora's expression before fading into the fog. But then, her grandmother had been a very proper lady who could swear like a sailor, so it shouldn't have come as a surprise. Cora turned and started walking back to where she'd entered. Without an anchor, she wouldn't have dared wander this far. The closer she was to the tear when she summoned Will, the faster she could leave. She could have spoken to other spirits, but she didn't know how much good it would do. And... Cyrus's family needed to know what happened.

It was little wonder they couldn't find him. To be killed here... he would be completely destroyed, both body and soul. There would be nothing left of him. Like he'd ceased to exist. The necromancer had done this. Cyrus must have been close to finding out their identity.

Just like that, the reality of what she was doing hit her. The necromancer had killed a reaper. Not to bring him back to life, but to protect their identity. She had to be more careful, or she could be killed, and her family would never find out what happened unless some spirit happened to be wandering by and saw what happened. This wasn't a horror story or a thriller. This was real. This was very, very real and there were consequences of getting involved.

Suddenly, she was afraid.

It took everything not to run for the tear and return to her body. She had to talk to Will. Just that, and then she could leave. She stopped, took a deep breath, and focused on Will. She knew the feel of his soul from going to his grave.

"Hello?"

She turned to face him. He was an older man, years older than Liam had been, though in the afterlife he stood straight and strong. "Will?"

He nodded, watching her eyes suspiciously. "What d'you want from me?"

"You were exorcised by someone I'm trying to find," she replied, "because you saw something he didn't want you to."

"I seen 'im wanderin' around the street not long after the family in the house across from me left on their trip. Kept 'is hood up, like he knew he was bein' watched. I saw 'im pick the lock to the house, seemed like he knew what he was doing." Will moved like he was going to spit on the ground, then glanced at her and stopped himself. "Never saw no one come out after, or anyone go in. But the next day I went to the edge of the yard, watching a couple 'a kids playin' hockey, and I seen him in the window, but all I could see was that he had short brown hair, and 'is eyes didn't glow like yours does." He frowned. "But when I was tossed through the Veil, I'm sure I seen 'is eyes glow, but the rest of 'is face was covered."

"Okay." That was something. "Do our eyes normally glow to you?"

He nodded, and she felt foolish for not knowing that already. "Not very bright, not like they glows over on this side, but there's something to 'em. Liam says its normal."

She frowned. Okay, that was significant. She put it to the back of her mind to focus on later and looked around when she heard the sound of another tear opening, like wind through chimes.

"That's been happening a lot lately," Will said, looking around. Perhaps he didn't see the world through the same fog she did.

"It's just reapers," she told him. "That's what it always sounds like when a tear opens, but it might not be close to us." It still served as a reminder that she needed to warn him that he could become a target.

"Right..."

"But you should be careful, all the same. The necromancer might come after you, afraid that someone like me will come by and ask questions about what you've seen. All the other ghosts who saw him were killed."

He frowned, confused. "I'm already dead."

"If you get stabbed with one of our knives your spirit will be destroyed, either here or in the land of the living."

"Oh." He sighed. "I gotta say, my death has been far more exciting than my life."

"Funny how that happens," she said.

Will nodded, then his eyes went wide as he caught sight of something behind her. That was all the warning she had. Cora twisted around, and by luck the blade of the dagger scored along her ribs instead of going through her heart. She gasped at the flare of agony that quickly faded, to be born by her physical body.

She found herself looking up at the necromancer, his glowing eyes full of a dark, twisted madness and guilt while a scarf hid the rest of his face.

"Who are you?" She demanded as she moved back, putting space between them and pulling Will back with her. He lunged at her instead of answering, which wasn't unexpected. She kept moving, trying to keep him focused on her, hoping Will would run the other way. Cora started running, trying to make it back to her body. If the necromancer tried to make a tear to follow her out, Jet would stop him. She didn't have any weapons as a spirit. She glanced back and stopped when she couldn't see the necromancer. Had he gone after Will instead? Was she far enough ahead that he was lost in the fog?

The soft sound of wind chimes made her turn again as the necromancer emerged through another tear, this time in front of her. What the hell? Using tears beyond the Veil? She hadn't known it was possible. She scrambled back as he lunged again, and then ducked his strike and stepped forward, trying to get close enough to rip away his scarf and reveal his identity. But the mad reaper reversed the blade and yanked it back. She tried to twist away, and the necromancer only managed to cut her upper arm before the blade sank into his side when he couldn't stop it, trapping Cora against him for a brief moment. She pushed back as he staggered, putting space between them again. He didn't seem to care that he'd injured himself, just glared at her as he ripped the bloody knife free from his own flesh with a grunt.

"Cora, run, I'll distract him!" She almost jumped out of her skin when she heard Will speak behind her. She hesitated, still trying to stay between the ghost and the necromancer. She should be protecting Will, not the other way around. It was her job, her duty. But she was unarmed, and the necromancer was out for blood. She couldn't win this fight. She felt torn, and frightened. Will gripped her uninjured arm and shoved her aside as the necromancer lunged again. "Run!"

She ran. Cora raced for the tear, for her body, for safety. She was close enough to see the glow when she looked back one more time. Through the gathering fog she could still see Will and the necromancer. She could see when Will was stabbed through the heart with a reaper's dagger. She watched as he dissipated into silver smoke, and the necromancer turned to face her again. If she'd had a heart in this form, it would have been pounding as she lunged through the tear before he could make another move, trusting her brother to close it as the weight of her physical body settled around her once more.

She was so very cold, except for the warmth spreading over her arm and her side, pain radiating through her. There was pressure on the wounds, making it worse, and her brother and Mike were talking in urgent tones. She could hear sirens in the distance. It was far too difficult to open her eyes, and Jet dropped her hands, gripping her shoulders, talking. But she couldn't make out the words. She was so tired, so cold, and in so much pain. The voices grew louder, and she closed her eyes, letting the darkness swallow her.

$$5$$

Cora woke up to a rhythmic beeping. Everything was fuzzy, like she was trying to swim through clouds in her mind, but they were slowly clearing away. She was cold, frozen, but any other pain was muted. She was aware that it should exist, but she couldn't feel it. There was someone holding her hand, though. She opened her eyes, blinking against the harsh lights and turned her head, blinking again to try to clear her vision while her mind scrambled to catch up.

"Cora?"

She finally focused on the speaker as things became clearer. "Dad?"

"I'm so glad you're awake." He reached over and hugged her. She could feel his arms shaking a little. Cora tried to return the embrace, but couldn't really move her arms, especially her left.

But there were more important things. "Where's Jet?" She had to tell him about Cyrus.

"Gone to the airport to pick up your mother," he replied, sitting down in one of the chairs by her bed again. "Lily just ran up to the vending machines to get something for us to eat."

"Mom's coming home?" Cora felt guilty, but at the same time, she was grateful.

"Yeah, her flight should be landing any minute now."

"Is someone else going to take over the investigation?" She had no idea if she wanted that or not.

"Lady Morrigan said that was up to you," he replied hesitantly. She tried to sit up but felt an odd pull along her side that made her grimace. It didn't hurt, not yet, it just felt weird in an uncomfortable way. "Hang on," her father said as he adjusted the bed. "You're gonna need a while to recover."

"He will too," she said, remembering the injury he'd inflicted on himself. "He stabbed himself while he was trying to kill me." Things she'd never thought she'd say. Someone had tried to kill her. Someone had genuinely *wanted* to *kill* her.

"Cora?" At her father's gentle and concerned tone, she realized that her hands were shaking badly.

"I'm fine," she answered as the door opened and Lily walked in.

"It's good to see you awake," she said, tossing a bag of chips and bottle of water to their father. "How do you feel?" Unlike Cora and Jet, she was human like their father, and a medium, her green eyes bright in the hospital lights.

She shrugged. "I don't really know. Fine? How am I supposed to feel about someone trying to kill me?"

"Fucked if I know," she replied with a shrug, ignoring the look their father gave her. "Jet and Mom are just waiting on her luggage," she added, sitting on the end of the bed and opening her own chips. "Did you find anything out to make it worthwhile?"

"Lily!"

"Yeah, maybe..." Cora swallowed hard. She remembered everything that had happened beyond the Veil. "I don't know. I got information, but someone died to protect me." She was certain Will was dead, destroyed. Truly gone and unable to enjoy the afterlife. Her father hugged her again and Lily patted her leg sympathetically. Maybe the necromancer would have gone after him anyway, but she couldn't help but feel like it was her fault. Maybe he never would have found Will if she hadn't gone searching for him. "I want to go home." Her voice cracked as she said it.

"Soon. As soon as the doctor says its okay," her father promised. Cora nodded, feeling more like a child than an adult with a career. One that now included lives being on the line.

"Does Maryanne know I'm here? How long have I been out?" Her housemate would worry.

"Well, you were beyond the Veil for most of yesterday, it was evening when you made it to the hospital, and now it's about five-ish, so a full day," Lily replied. "I called her, though. She knows."

Cora nodded. "Thanks. And... what about Emily?"

Lily sighed. "Maryanne called her after we hung up. She was here last night, and she said she'd come back after work. So, soon, actually. But you should send her a message or something to let her know you're awake."

"Is she mad?"

"Because you didn't tell her you were going to do something dangerous and then got hurt very badly and she had to hear all of this from Maryanne?"

Cora looked away. "Yeah..."

"She's worried, and scared, and yeah, she's mad," Lily replied. "But its mostly worry."

"I was trying to keep her from worrying..." Cora said quietly, hands gripping the blankets piled around her.

"Cora... you should have told her," their father said gently. "Speaking from experience, its better to know and be able to worry. Then at least we can know that you're trying to be safe. I know its hard, but you shouldn't do that to people you care about."

"I know, but..." she trailed off, uncertain of how to finish that thought. She'd blame the drugs.

"She's nothing like Hannah," Lily pointed out. "She won't do anything like that to you." Cora looked away again, shrinking back against the bed.

"Try to get some rest," their father said. "We can talk about this later."

Cora nodded and tried to relax until her mother and Jet came barging into the room. Her mother hugged her carefully, and Cora, once again, tried to return the embrace. It was a little easier this time. She looked over at her brother. There were dark circles around his eyes, and the grey strands in his dark hair seemed to stand out more than usual.

"Cyrus is dead," she told him, her voice cracking. "The necromancer killed him beyond the Veil."

Her brother stared at her for a long moment, not saying anything.

"He was innocent." She hated that she could feel tears rolling down her cheeks.

Jet nodded once, then walked out of the room. Their father followed him, and Lily handed her a tissue so she could wipe her eyes.

"You can hand the case over to someone else if you want. No one would blame you," her mother said, an echo of her father's words.

Part of her wanted to. Part of her wanted to wash her hands of the danger, wanted to be safe. But the necromancer would probably still try to hunt her down, because she knew too much. On top of that, she would be putting someone else in the line of fire. How many people would she allow to get between her and danger? One had so far, and he was gone now. Already, that seemed like too much. Could she handle the guilt of another? It was far too heavy a question for her to handle right now.

"I just want to go home," she said instead of answering, curling up as much as she could, wishing she could feel warm again.

"Soon," her mother said. "We'll get you home, and you can update the case files while its still fresh in your memory."

Cora nodded. "Whoever it is wears contacts sometimes," she said. "Will... he said the necromancer's eyes didn't glow when he saw him in the window."

Lily frowned. "Glow?"

"Our eyes glow to ghosts on this plane and to spirits on the next," their mother explained absently. "That could be useful information."

"And he's using the Veil to travel, to get his victims to the houses and then to the harbour in the dories. He even used tears within the Veil."

"Clever, but dangerous."

"And he's injured." She explained how he'd injured himself.

"I'll look into anyone who came in looking for treatment," her mother said. "But I doubt he did. You try to get some rest, okay?"

Cora nodded and closed her eyes again, the drugs ensuring she fell asleep quickly.

When Cora opened her eyes, she wasn't alone. Just as her sister had promised. Lily was still sitting on the end of her bed, and Emily was occupying the seat beside her, holding her hand. Her girlfriend's eyes were red and puffy, like she'd been crying, and she looked like she hadn't been sleeping.

"Hey," Cora said, resisting the urge to feign sleep like a coward. Emily looked up from their hands.

"Hey." She untangled their fingers to reach over and brush a lock of Cora's hair behind her ear. "How do you feel?"

"Okay, I guess," she replied. She couldn't feel her wounds, at least.

"I'm gonna go get some coffee," Lily decided, looking between them. "Dad had to go to work, Mom ordered Jet to get some rest, and she's on the phone outside."

"Don't you need to go to work?"

She shrugged. "They let me have the day off when I called." She worked for their family line in record keeping. She reached over and gently squeezed Cora's good shoulder before getting up and leaving the couple alone. Cora turned her head to face Emily again, unsure of what to say.

Emily was the one to break the silence. "I had to find out that you were not only in hospital from your dead housemate, but you were also doing dangerous shit and keeping it secret from me." She leaned back in her chair, crossing her arms. Lily was right, she was mad.

"I'm sorry..." Cora hated how weak her voice sounded to her own ears.

"Don't you trust me?" Emily asked, her eyes glassy with tear as her voice broke. "I told you I wasn't going to run screaming. Why don't you believe me?" Cora felt even more guilty than she had before.

"I do trust you," she argued, even though she knew there were many flaws in that argument.

"Then why not tell me when you were going to do something risky?" She demanded. "I know I can't be there to help you, you need another reaper, but... I could be there with Maryanne to help you when you get home." Emily clenched her hands into fists.

"I didn't want you to worry." The argument had sounded bad when she said it to Maryanne. It sounded even worse saying it to her girlfriend. "I was wrong to do it. I'm sorry."

"Do you have any idea what its like? I thought you were fine, not doing anything that could kill you or take days to recover from, and then I find out that not only are you in the fucking *hospital*, but that it would take you days to recover from what you were doing *anyway*!" She paused to take a breath, visibly trying to calm down a little before she spoke again. "When were you going to tell me?"

"When you called or sent a text after I got home," Cora replied, curling up a little despite her efforts not to.

Emily wiped her eyes with the sleeve of her sweater. "I think I deserve more than that, Cora."

She swallowed hard and nodded. "You're right, I know you're right... it's just... I've been burned. Badly." She didn't want to think of Hannah now, though.

"I understand. But I love you just the way you are, Cora, and I hope you'll remember that next time."

Cora couldn't help but stare. Love? Had she really heard that right? Looking at her, Cora thought that maybe she had. "Really?" The question came out before she could stop it.

Emily nodded. "Yes. I'm mad at you right now, but I love you." She leaned over and kissed her gently. "And I don't want to lose you."

"I love you too." Her voice was rough with emotion.

There was a knock on the door before a doctor entered. Emily sat down again as Cora was subjected to a round of tests she didn't really understand, and her mother returned to explain what was normal for reapers in Cora's situation. After what felt like an eternity, they decided she could finally go home.

"I'm going to make a quick run home to grab a few things before I head to your place, okay?" Emily asked, pulling on her coat.

Cora nodded, and Emily said polite goodbyes to Cora's mother and sister before leaving. It was then she realized that this was the first time her mother was meeting her girlfriend.

"I like her," her mother remarked as the door closed. "Did you two have a chance to talk?"

Cora nodded as she struggled into the clothes that Lily had brought over, then figured out the sling she would need to wear while her arm healed. "Yeah, we worked things out."

"Good." Between the three of them she made it to her sister's car and survived the trip home.

"I'm so glad you're alright!" Maryanne exclaimed as they walked inside, Cora leaning heavily against Lily. Whatever they'd given her at the hospital had been very strong. "I was so worried."

"Thanks."

"The detective keeps calling. He said he tried to get Alan but there was no answer."

"Oh," Lily broke in, "Alan had to head home to Alberta. There was some kind of family emergency. He told Jet yesterday after he couldn't get Cora. He'll call as soon as he can."

"Ah, well, I hope everything is alright," she said, then looked back at Cora. "Did you see Emily?" Despite her concern, there was still a hint of disapproval in her gaze.

She nodded. "We talked. I won't do that again." She'd only gone from St Clair's to home, but she felt exhausted and frozen, and the drugs were messing with her head a little when upright. "I think I'm gonna lie down for a bit."

"I'll bring up some hot water bottles," Maryanne offered.

"Thanks." Her mother helped her get upstairs, where Maryanne had left a pile of blankets on her bed.

"You should probably call the detective before you get too comfortable."

"Right..."

"And he'll probably want to know if you're going to continue the investigation."

Shit. "Yeah..."

"Do you know what you want to do? I know its not an easy decision, but we don't have time to wait, even if the necromancer is injured."

She took a deep breath. "I'm staying on the case." No one else needed to be put in danger.

Her mother watched her expression closely. "Are you sure?"

She nodded with more conviction than she felt. "Yes."

"Okay." Her mother located her cell phone and handed it over before heading downstairs. Cora took a deep breath to brace herself and selected Mike from her contacts. It only rang twice before he picked up.

"Cora?"

"No 'Detective Byrne?'" She wondered.

That got her a chuckle that sounded more like relief than finding her humorous. "How are you?"

"Alright, tired. I just got home."

"That's good. You gave us a hell of a fright." She could imagine. Watching wounds appear when there was no apparent cause would be terrifying. "You still on the case?"

"Yeah..." That sounded too uncertain. "Yeah, I am."

"Good." There was sincere relief in his voice. "D'you know what happened to that buddy of yours? I tried calling him, but there was no answer."

"Apparently he had to go back to Alberta for some kind of family emergency," she replied. "I'll try to find out when he's supposed to get back."

"Okay. I know you probably just want to rest, but I need to know if there's, well, anything I need to know."

"Cyrus is off the suspect list, and this case is definitely over your head." She explained how the necromancer was using the Veil as a means of transportation, and that they would likely have a short reprieve because he was injured.

"Maybe we are in over our heads, but we won't stop," Mike promised. "Get some rest, I'll do another sweep of the first neighbourhood, see if the neighbours have anything to say. I won't mention the murders, but I'd like to solve this before we have another body on our hands."

"Okay." They hung up. Then Cora remembered that Cyrus's family and the heads of both families would need to know about his death. She didn't know if she could handle that.

There was a knock on the door, and her mother entered again with the hot water bottles Maryanne had promised. "How'd everything go?"

"Fine... I have to tell Cyrus's parents what happened, don't I?"

"Your brother took care of that," she replied gently, settling the hot water bottles around Cora. "Lady Morrigan will need to be told, but you can rest first. She'll contact Lord Viduus, though he'll likely hear from Cyrus's family before then, and then call her. One way or another everyone who needs to know will find out."

"Okay." She curled up as much as she could, hoping she'd start to feel warm soon. Her mother tucked her in like she had when Cora was a child before heading downstairs. It wasn't long before Cora discovered something new: she was afraid of being alone. Even here, in her own home, she was waiting for the air to split open, revealing that silver glow and the necromancer there to finish what he'd started. She could hear talking downstairs, but that did nothing to comfort her. Like a child, she pulled the blankets up higher, as if they would protect her.

She wasn't sure how long she lay there, trying to figure out what to do, when the door opened and she nearly jumped out of her skin. "You okay?" Emily asked, frowning at her reaction.

"How long is it gonna be before that's not the first thing people say to me again?" She asked instead of answering, trying for dry humour and failing miserably.

Emily was clearly not amused. "Cora."

She shifted uncomfortably under the blankets. "I'm scared," she admitted at last. "I'm scared he's going to come after me while I'm sleeping or alone." She looked away, then back at Emily. "I'm supposed to feel safe in my own home, aren't I? So why don't I?"

Emily put her bag down and crossed the room to the bed. "Well, something scary just happened when you were alone, so its kind of make sense to feel that way. But you're not alone now. I'm here, Maryanne is here, and your family isn't about to leave you unprotected." She gave her a slight smile. "You won't be alone. And you're still the big, badass reaper, even if you need help for a little while."

Cora managed a weak smile. "Thanks." She shuffled over in the bed as much as she could. Emily settled on top of the covers, claiming Cora was too much of an icicle, which was fair. It made her a little guilty how good it felt having another person there. What if the necromancer appeared and went after Emily? Her thoughts started to spiral into dark places.

"Cora?" Cora looked over to meet Emily's gaze, wondering what in her expression gave it away. "Wherever your mind is going, *stop*. I'm here because I want to be."

"Okay." She shuffled a little closer to Emily before closing her eyes and letting herself drift off to sleep.

Then she woke up screaming from a nightmare. The necromancer's hands had been around her throat, choking her as she struggled to get away. After Emily and her mother helped her calm down, she realized that sleeping in a sling was a terrible idea, as the strap had pressed down on her neck. More painkillers followed, and she managed to sleep a little while longer once the sling was removed. However, it seemed she was doomed to relive the attack in her dreams, and what else could have gone horribly wrong.

The next time she woke gasping, her brother was sitting at her bedside. Emily was still curled up against her side. He looked even more like hell than he had at the hospital, with dark rings around his bloodshot eyes.

"Hey," he said.

"I'll go get tea," Emily decided, getting up. "Do either of you want any?"

"No thanks, I can't stay long," Jet said.

"Please," Cora said. Emily nodded and left, and Cora turned to her brother. "You okay?"

His expression turned wry. "Shouldn't I be asking you that?"

She shrugged and winced as pain radiated through her wounds. Apparently, the hospital-grade drugs were wearing off, and she was stuck with whatever the doctors had sent home with her. "Everyone's been asking me."

"I'll live," he replied, grimacing slightly. "I mean, we kinda knew this would be the outcome when he went missing."

"Doesn't mean it's easier," she pointed out. "You still had hope."

He shrugged. "It doesn't matter now. Nothing can bring him back." He sighed and ran a hand over his face. "But I guess I kinda get it now, you know? Why someone would be so desperate to bring the dead back to life."

"Jet..."

"Don't worry, I know better than to try." He fell silent for a moment but spoke before she could figure out what to say. "They're waiting to have his funeral until after Halloween. There's no body, so its not like they have to rush before it decomposes."

"Are you gonna go?"

"I'm thinking about it. If you catch the necromancer I will." He crossed his arms over his chest and leaned back in his chair. "You know, we were talking about visiting each other in a few months. We were just working on who'd be the one flying out... I was gonna ask him to be my best man."

"Jet..." She wasn't sure what to tell her brother. If he'd been a stranger it would have been easier to figure out the right thing to say.

"Don't worry about it, Cora. You've got enough on your plate." He managed a weak smile. "I'm just glad I didn't lose you too."

She reached out to her brother and he hugged her tight. "I'm not going anywhere," she promised.

"I know." She wasn't sure he believed it. But why would he? Cyrus was dead, and his killer had nearly killed *her*. "Alan said he'd call in a day or two. Seemed to think he was onto something." He let her go and sat down again.

"He's seemed pretty optimistic about his algorithm stuff," she said, curling up under her blankets again, trying to get warm among the hot water bottles, heating pads, and quilts.

Jet shrugged. "He seemed a bit... out of it when I was talking to him. More than usual. But we've all been under a lot of stress over the last week." Cora wasn't sure which was more surprising: that a full week had already gone by, or that it had *only* been a week.

"He does seem to have a bad coffee habit."

"That too. I've seen him drink six espresso shots in three hours and act like it was nothing." Jet stood and stretched. "I'll let your girlfriend back in, I know you'd rather cuddle with her." He smirked as he added that.

Cora glared, irritated that she couldn't throw a pillow right now. Jet's grin grew into a smirk. "Don't get so smug, I *will* have my revenge." Or Maryanne would have it for her. She was certain she could talk her housemate into it, even if it meant that a room was getting redecorated.

"I'm sure you will." His expression remained smug as he reached over and ruffled her hair while she couldn't retaliate before leaving. Just like that, ripping up the floor in the bathroom and re-tiling it seemed worth petty vengeance.

Emily wasn't long in returning. "Your brother seems a bit more cheerful, at least," she remarked, carefully handing over a mug of tea. Somehow Cora kept her good hand steady enough to hold it.

"Pissing me off has that effect on him," she grumbled, sipping her tea. The heat was comfortable and helped push the cold away. Emily chuckled and Cora gave her a look of betrayal.

Her girlfriend responded by kissing her. "You're being a good sister, helping to cheer him up." She knew Emily was still mad at her, still disappointed by the lie, but it did seem like they were going to be able to get past it.

"I know I'm the favourite," Cora said with a lofty drawl, though it would have been far more effective with Lily there. Emily snorted and settled in next to her, holding her close when she put the mug down and curled up again.

6

Though they'd all hoped for a few days to rest, it wasn't meant to be. Two nights later another body was found in the harbour. Cora made her way down to the crime scene, gripping the steering wheel tight so she didn't need to acknowledge how badly her hands were shaking. It had taken a long time to convince her mother and her housemate that she was fine to drive down on her own, let alone be at the crime scene. While she did have to be careful to keep from tearing her stitches, she couldn't afford to slack off anymore. Not when people were still dying.

"You sure you're up for this?" Mike asked as she got out of her car, shivering as the cold air hit her. She still hadn't quite warmed up again.

Cora barely remembered to shrug with one shoulder. "He has to be stopped." She wasn't going to put anyone else in danger.

Mike still looked skeptical. "Okay. This one is different than the others. Looks rushed to me." He led the way over to the dory, this one a deep green and bright pink. She could see Mike's point when they got close. The other bodies had been carved into with careful, almost mathematical precision. This one... the lines weren't quite as even; the flesh didn't seem to have been cut with as much care.

"Any ballpark on time of death?" Was it before or after the incident beyond the Veil?

Mike shook his head. "Not until we get to the morgue. Looks like the body was refrigerated, which slowed decomp. My best guess is that we're gonna find this one was killed just after you were attacked. We'll know more after the autopsy."

She nodded and took the pictures she needed, ditching the sling because she needed both hands. It was hard to keep her camera steady, and the pictures had to be as clear as possible. The same blade that had killed this man and carved a sick, twisted spell into his skin had nearly killed her just a few days before. Her wounds suddenly hurt a lot more.

"It's probably because Halloween is in three days," she replied, forcing herself to focus. "We'll probably start finding a lot more bodies while he tries to 'perfect' his method."

And she'd nearly been one of his victims.

She had to stop thinking like that.

"What do you expect for Halloween?"

An important and terrible question. "I'm not sure. I think he'll want to be at the Queen's Road tear and try something there. But my family owns the house, and he shouldn't be able to get past our security, even using the Veil to travel.

"Would it be better to wait until Halloween and lay a trap for him?"

She shook her head. "It'll be too crazy. Any spirit with thoughts of coming back will be trying to get through. Mom and Jet will be there. He'd be a fool to actually try anything."

"Okay..."

"Byrne, we got a possible match on ID," one of the techs said, leaning over a computer. "Gregory Callahan, thirty-six, works in IT at..." he trailed off for a moment, looking down at the screen again. When he said the company name, Cora felt the colour drain from her face.

"Cora?" Mike moved closer, clearly expecting her to collapse.

"Emily works there, with the IT department," she replied, her voice barely above a whisper.

"We'll need someone to give us a positive ID," the tech added.

"She knows what's going on," Cora told Mike. He looked hesitant and she forced herself to stand straighter, putting steel in her spine and in her voice. "Remember, this isn't really an RNC case. Provincial and federal laws don't apply the same. Our laws come first." Which was why she wouldn't be tried for murder when she brought the necromancer down. It was an execution, a sanctioned murder.

He sighed but didn't argue. "Do you want her on the scene or at the morgue?"

"Morgue," she replied. Then the marks would be hidden and Emily wouldn't have to see them.

"Okay. I'll have someone let you know when the body's ready. I have to appear at a trial soon, so it'll probably be another detective there, but I'll give you a number to reach me if they give you any trouble." Not everyone was as willing to work with a reaper as he was.

"Thanks." She turned and headed back to her car, beating her fist off the steering wheel before putting it into drive and swallowing a scream of frustration. She should have done *something* beyond the Veil. She wasn't powerless. She wasn't supposed to be helpless. Maybe she could have saved George Callahan if she hadn't run, if she'd tried to fight.

She waited until she got home to call Emily.

"Cora? Is something wrong?"

"Yeah... I need you this afternoon... its about the case. Sorry, I don't want to say much over the phone." Phones weren't immune from being hacked. And she had to remember that the necromancer was probably a fair hand with technology, getting at people's travel information.

"That's fine, I think I can get away. We've been down a person for a few days, so it's been... busy...." Cora knew she'd put the pieces together when her voice trailed off. "Cora..."

"I... can't say anything over the phone," she insisted.

"Okay... what time?"

"I'll pick you up at two? Or would you rather drive yourself?"

"I'll take my car home and you can pick me up there?"

"Okay."

"I'll call if something comes up." Emily was clearly trying to mask how upset she was.

"Okay... Emily, I'm sorry."

"No, this isn't your fault, Cora. I'll see you later." She hung up.

Cora put the phone down. He'd been missing a few days. That was something. It meant that his death might not have been prevented by her running instead of fighting. At least, that's what she tried to tell herself. As pathetic as it was. She got a shower and then got Maryanne's help replacing her bandages. She didn't know where her mother had gone. The wounds remained a few degrees colder than the rest of her skin, and the scars would always be like that, though she would get used to it. Scars etched on her skin and in her soul forever, permanent reminders of what had happened. That was what she'd been told, anyway. The cut she'd made with her own blade wasn't deep enough to leave a scar and would heal completely.

Her mind spiralled from there, to the woman she loved. George Callahan worked with Emily. The IT department all shared an office. If George had been taken there, Emily could have just as easily become a victim. So far there was no pattern in the necromancer's victims. They couldn't tell if any of them were planned or if he was just an opportunist. Unless George was a warning, because he worked with Emily? It wouldn't take much to find out that Emily was Cora's girlfriend, especially if the necromancer was as good with computers as they thought.

"Cora?" She jumped a little, and then looked at Maryanne, wondering how long she'd been spacing out.

"Sorry." She gave herself a mental shake.

"Penny for your thoughts?"

"It's a nickle now. We got rid of the penny, remember?" It was admittedly a poor attempt at humour. Maryanne raised a brow. Cora sighed, tapping her fingers against the table. "I was just thinking... Emily and George shared an office. The necromancer could have taken her."

"Was he taken at work?"

"I don't know. I just... it's still too close." She looked up at her housemate. "Is it bad that I'm happy it wasn't her?"

Maryanne thought for a moment. "No. I'd say it's normal. Espeically after everything that's happened."

"Right..." But she still felt guilty. There was still a family, friends, loved ones who would be grieving. She'd gotten lucky this time. But she had to remember, no one was safe. Not until she ended this.

"Hey," Cora said as Emily got into the passenger seat.

"Tell me, is it what I think it is?" She asked without preamble, looking at Cora.

She couldn't look away from those dark brown eyes. "There was another victim. One of the tech's ID'd him, but we need someone to confirm. It does look like it's George Callahan. You work with him and you know about the case, so you're the best person to do it."

Emily took a deep breath. "I can do that." Her voice shook as she spoke. Cora started driving and slowly reached over to hold her hand, giving her a chance to pull away. She didn't, thankfully. In truth Cora needed the contact just as much.

"You'll only have to see his face," Cora promised.

"It's okay. I... I didn't tell anyone at work." She pulled a tissue out of her pocket to wipe her eyes. Cora nodded. It would be better for the family to find out before others. They didn't talk much for the rest of the drive, though the silence wasn't uncomfortable. The parking at the Health Sciences building was as crazy as ever, but she managed to get reasonably close to the front doors.

"Where are we meeting Mike?" Emily wondered, sticking close as they entered. Cora got some looks for wearing sunglasses inside, but she'd found out long ago that patients and their families tended to get even more nervous than usual around reapers. She couldn't really say she blamed them.

"We're not meeting Mike, we're meeting..." she checked her phone, "Detective John Murphy."

"Is that someone you've worked with before?"

She shook her head. "I don't think so. I might have met him in passing? Jet'd probably know. Or Mom." She sent them both a message asking if either knew him. She got a reply before they made it to the morgue.

"Well?" Emily asked.

"Jet says no, Mom says she's only met him in passing."

"I guess we'll find out for ourselves." She was clearly trying to put on a brave face. Cora put her phone back in her pocket and reached over to hold her hand, tangling their fingers together. She wanted to say that everything would be okay, but it felt like a lie.

The detective was waiting for them outside of the morgue. He was older, probably in his fifties and only slightly taller than Cora. The instant she met his gaze she knew there would be problems. His disdain for her was clear.

"Detective Murphy?" She kept her tone polite.

"You're the reaper?" He asked, looking from her to Emily, who tensed beside her.

She took off her sunglasses and put them in her pocket, meeting his gaze steadily. He flinched. "Cora Morrigan," she introduced herself, holding out her hand. Detective Murphy shook it with clear reluctance, and she forced herself to keep a polite expression. "And this is Emily Tailor, here to identify the victim." Emily shook the detective's hand as well.

"This isn't normal protocol," he remarked.

"This isn't a normal case," she replied. "I'm sure that Detective Byrne told you what you needed to know?"

"He told me what he believed I needed to know. But a lot of this doesn't make sense. There are policies for a reason and we can't just make exceptions to them."

She gave him a smile that was polite, but cool. "If you have any questions you can refer to your superiors."

"I have," he informed her.

"Then why are we wasting time here?" She wondered. Despite her insecurities, when Cora was on duty, she knew her duty, she knew what was at stake, and she had the pride of her family lineage to put steel in her spine. The detective seemed surprised that she wasn't intimidated. She raised a brow when he didn't answer, and the detective scowled as he led them into the morgue.

"You're not going to do anything... freaky with the body, are you?" He asked.

She gave him a carefully neutral look. "What do you mean by that?"

"You know..." he trailed off.

"Clearly not." She glanced back at Emily to make sure she was okay. Her girlfriend gave her a weak smile. "But whatever your concerns may be, I'm only here for the identification. Though if you'd like, I can have information on what we actually do sent to your office so you can educate yourself."

"Not necessary," he snapped. A doctor joined them, and they were led to an examination room. The body was laid out on a metal table and covered with a sheet. The doctor pulled it back so only the face was visible.

Emily pressed close to Cora as she looked at the body, her breath catching. "That's him," she managed to say, clinging to Cora. It was almost funny, leaning on a reaper for comfort in the face of death. "That's George."

"Okay." The doctor covered him again, which seemed a bit odd, but then, Emily wasn't a reaper. They'd never felt the need to hide a body from Cora's sight.

"Is there anything else you need here?" The detective demanded in a sharp tone, watching her closely.

"No, there isn't," she replied as she slipped an arm around Emily's waist and put her sunglasses back on. There was nothing to gain in being antagonistic. Instead she ignored the disapproving gaze of the detective and gently led her girlfriend out of the morgue.

They just made it out of the building before Emily broke down, sobbing. Cora pulled her over to a bench so they could sit, and held her tight, ignoring the ache of her healing wounds. It would be different for her; she should have remembered that. Emily was tough as hell, but she wasn't used to seeing bodies, let alone the bodies of her murdered coworkers. Cora was numb to all of that. She hummed a random tune, trying to be comforting. People kept walking past, most ignoring them completely.

"I'm okay," Emily rasped eventually. "It's just..."

"It's fine, you don't have to explain," Cora said, rubbing her back. "I should have warned you."

"He's gone. Is his soul..."

"I'll find it and I'll make sure he makes it into the afterlife," she promised quietly. What would she do if it was Emily in the dory one day? If she had to see her face under the sheet, the ritualistic marks carved into her skin? She barely repressed a shudder. "I'll stop this. I'll stop him. I swear." Maybe she should admit her fears and her guilt to Emily, but this wasn't the time to do it.

"Can we go?" Emily asked a few moments later.

"Yeah, we can go," she agreed, standing carefully.

Emily dried her eyes with her jacket sleeve. "Do you mind if I spend the night at your place? I... I don't think I want to be alone tonight."

"Of course." Her phone buzzed and she pulled it out of her pocket. It was from Alan, letting her know he was back in town. "I have to talk to Alan, since he's back, but that probably won't take long."

"Okay. I have some errands I should probably run," she said as they got into the car. "I'll see if Maryanne wants anything picked up. Seems the least I can do, since I'm spending half the time at your place anyway."

It was on the tip of Cora's tongue to suggest she move in, but like many things, now wasn't the time. "I'm sure she'll appreciate it." She sent Alan a reply and made her way out of the parking lot and back into the afternoon traffic.

Emily was silent until she got to a red light by the mall. "Cora..."

Her tone had Cora glancing over. "Yeah?"

"Do... do you think he might come after me?" There was fear in her eyes. It wasn't fair. Emily shouldn't be part of this.

She forced her eyes back onto the road, gripping the steering wheel with white knuckles. "I don't know. It's possible." She wanted to glance over but couldn't bring herself to.

"Okay." There was a quiet, resigned, acceptance in her voice.

"Em..."

"I'm not going to leave you," Emily added. Now Cora did glance over. Emily looked determined. "Just... until you catch him, can I stay at your place? I'm probably safer with Maryanne than on my own."

"Yeah..." She always expected the worst, and it never happened. Not with Emily. "That's a good idea. Mom said she'd probably split her time between home and my place until I regain full use of my arm." Given the way she was treating her injuries at the moment, that would probably be a while.

"Okay." Emily reached over to put her hand on Cora's leg. "Just promise me you'll stay safe, okay?"

"Only if you'll promise me the same thing," she replied.

Emily managed a weak smile. "I'll do my best."

"Then so will I." She just hoped it was a promise she could keep.

Cora checked her phone before she pulled away from Emily's place. Alan had messaged her again, letting her know when he would be at the university later. It was just as well, since she wanted to look into a few things first, namely the progress being made in clearing reapers. It had been a while since she'd checked.

Her mother was home when she returned. "How did everything go?"

"Emily is going to stay here for a few days," she replied. "She identified the latest victim."

"I'll have some tea for her," Maryanne said. "You know, death isn't what it used to be. It wasn't so hidden away in hospitals and funeral homes. We'd wake our dead at home. It was less scary back then."

"Well, times have changed," Cora's mother said with a sigh. "And we just have to do our part to try to change things for the better. Is Emily alright?"

"She's shaken, and... she's worried the necromancer might target her next."

"We'll make sure she's safe here." It wasn't an assurance that Emily's fears, that her own fears, were wrong, that there was nothing to worry about.

"Thanks. I'm going to see if there's any updates on who's been cleared, since it seems like no one has been seen as suspicious."

"Good idea."

"Have you heard from Jet today?" Because Emily wasn't the only one reeling from a death connected to the case.

Her mother gave her a sad smile. "I was over at his place earlier. He's doing the best he can, but this is hard on him. If you called him later, I'm sure he'd appreciate hearing from you."

Cora nodded, trying to push down her fears for Emily when they tried to take over her mind again. She headed upstairs and logged onto the reaper network. There was a message from the network admin that they were still looking into who had logged in with Cyrus's information, but that was from two days ago. She accessed a private folder that showed who was cleared and who still had to be investigated. Her family had been cleared already, and it looked like most of the active reapers had, with two marked as suspicious. One of them had moved from Toronto to Fredericton recently. New Brunswick was close, especially when travelling through tears. They were starting on the inactive reapers now, like Alan. Oddly enough, he seemed to be at the bottom of the list despite being in St John's. But then, he was helping her.

She glanced at a few other names, looking for people she knew among the names cleared, wanting to make sure they were there. She didn't want to have to kill them. Taking a life wasn't what her job was meant to be, but if it had to be done... was it terrible to hope it was a stranger? Or at least, someone she'd only met in passing?

Curiosity got the best of her, and she opened her own file. It had a surprising amount of information. Physical details, her medical records, psychological assessments, even her academic records. Everything compiled in one location. Those responsible for combing the records had a huge job ahead of them, looking at every detail, trying to assess if it meant something or not. And any mistake would make the pile of bodies grow.

Cora closed her eyes for a moment. It was time to think like a detective, like someone who had to solve a string of grisly murders before another corpse ended up on her conscience. Which was exactly the situation she was in. She pulled out her notebook and looked through her file. The records contained details about her dagger, and even mentioned that she wore sunglasses in public places. Then she checked Alan's, because she knew he wore contacts, and found that was noted as well. Backing out of the file, she typed in contact lenses to narrow the search. The list reduced dramatically. Well then. She tried a few other combinations, but other than the type of stone on the dagger, nothing else she knew made much of a difference. She remembered the necromancer used turquoise in his pommel, but it wasn't an uncommon choice

There was still time before she had to meet Alan, so she typed up her report for Lady Morrigan on George Callahan. She thought about contacting Cyrus's family, it seemed like the right thing to do, but truth be told, she had no idea what she'd say to them. Anything she could think of didn't seem right, not when his murderer was still on the loose.

Cora found a parking spot near the Mun library and claimed it, taking a moment to gather her thoughts and down a few ibuprofen. Her mother hadn't been thrilled about her driving more, but Cora knew she still had things to do related to her work in Japan and insisted that she was fine on her own. Even though she wasn't on many levels.

How did Mike do it? He'd worked in homicide for most of his career. The people she dealt with were already dead, ghosts and poltergeists. She didn't deal directly with murderers and the direct aftermath of their crimes. As much as their worlds were connected, she dealt with something very different, and she wanted to go back to that.

"Hey," Alan greeted her as when she approached the counter. He looked as tired as she felt, pale with dark circles around his bloodshot eyes. Not even contacts could hide that.

"Hey. How did everything go with your family?"

He shrugged with his left shoulder. "Could be better. Doesn't help that I slipped on ice right before getting on the plane, so my side is messed up. Though I suppose my injuries still aren't as bad as yours." He managed a wry grin, but it didn't reach his eyes.

She responded with a grin of her own. "I didn't realize word would get around so quickly. Did you see a doctor?"

"Yeah, just some strained muscles," he said, waving away her concern before adjusting his sweater, pulling it higher over his neck. "How are you doing?"

"Alright," she replied, deciding to stay vague. "I'll probably lie down when I get home, though. Did you find out anything new?"

"Sorry, the lead I thought I had fell apart." He grimaced. "I guess I could have just said as much in a message, couldn't I?" He picked up a mug and drank deeply, then looked into it and sighed. "Why don't we get coffee and talk?"

"Sure... but wouldn't it be better for you to take a day off and sleep? You must be finding the jet lag hard."

He stared at her for a moment before the words seemed to fully register. "Yes, probably. But there's a lot of work to be done, and time is growing short." He gave another jerky shrug with one shoulder before leading the way out of the library. Cora caught up, walking alongside him. "Besides, there's a necromancer on the lose."

"That's my headache," Cora reminded him.

"Well, yes, but its all anyone is worried about, especially with Cyrus dead."

Cora blinked. "Word gets around fast." As far as she knew, only Lord Viduus and Cyrus's immediate family had been told. They were being given a few days before letting everyone know.

"Oh... Jet told me earlier."

"Okay..." She knew he'd talked to her brother before she'd woken up, but chances were they'd spoken recently as well.

"Shame, really, Cyrus was a great guy." The sincerity of his words caught her before she could go farther down that rabbit hole, and she looked over at him.

"I didn't realize you were close."

"I don't know if I'd call us close, but I spent a few years in Toronto before I moved here," he replied. "We got to know each other while I was training to work in the archives and records. I've thought about going back once I finish my doctorate... but I think I might go home to Alberta. It's been an age since I spent any amount of time there."

She'd been under the impression he went back often. Something wasn't adding up, and it was starting to scare her. Their conversation dropped while they ordered his coffee with a lot of added espresso and her tea. She tried to watch him surreptitiously. Jet was right, something was off, even if they were all stressed. In the light of the sun it looked almost like he was wearing makeup, like a fine layer of foundation, but not all over his face. Had he always worn makeup? But why not try to hide the circles around his eyes? It was hard to ignore the fact that one of the later symptoms necromancers experienced was their veins becoming more visible, and darker. She tried to mask her unease as they headed back outside instead of taking the walkways and tunnels that led to all the buildings.

"D'you mind if I ask why you left? It sounds like you miss it."

Again there was a pause, like it took a few moments for the words to fully process, and he looked at her for a moment, like he was making up his mind about something. "It's the same reason I switched from reaping to researching," he replied, taking a sip of coffee. She had no idea how he could drink that. "I... I messed up. Badly." He paused for another moment, and she could tell that whatever happened still weighed on him. "There were two kids haunting a park that wasn't far from Edmonton. They'd been there for a few years, not all that long. My family found out and I was sent out to deal with it." He swallowed hard and sat down on a bench. Cora followed. "They were so young, Cora. I don't think either of them were over ten. I tried to find out what happened to them, how they'd died, but they couldn't tell me anything. They were lost and scared and lonely." He tugged at his sweater.

"I find kids the hardest to deal with," she admitted, remember the boy, Jack, from a week ago. Before all of this started.

Alan nodded. "They asked for a few more days, just to say goodbye to everyone and everything. I shouldn't have... but I said okay. I took their names and I went home. I thought that if I could find anything about what had happened to them, it would help them move on." He rubbed a hand over his face.

"Did you find anything out?"

"No, I didn't. And a few days later I found out they'd gone from ghosts to poltergeists and killed a child, so it could join them forever," he said bitterly. "Its not fair. None of them deserved that."

"You're right, but that's how it is," Cora said, very lightly bumping her shoulder against his in a comforting gesture as she sipped her tea.

"Its not right," he insisted, his empty hand closing into a white-knuckled fist, before he glanced at her concerned expression and took a deep breath, visibly struggling to relax. "Anyway, I couldn't handle any more cases after that, and I switched to research. Someone else had to be sent to deal with the children in the park."

"I'm sorry that happened." She didn't really know what to say. It was a tragedy.

"Me too... I should probably get back to work," he said, standing abruptly. Cora thought his eyes looked glassy. He looked shaken, and he grimaced, putting his hand over his left side, as if putting pressure on a wound that ached.

She stood slowly in an effort to avoid doing the same. "Okay. Look, why don't you take it easy? Call me if you think on anything, but don't make it a priority."

"Alright. Take care." He adjusted his sweater again, pulling it higher around his neck. "I wish none of this had come to... well... this."

"Same." She watched as he walked away before heading to her car. As she sat down, she took a deep breath, trying to sort through all the emotions that bombarded her.

She had a suspect. Now she just needed proof. If she decided someone was guilty, they would be killed. By her. She would be responsible for taking a life. Even if he'd attacked her and tried to kill her, she wasn't an executioner. Hell, she could sympathize with what would drive someone down this road. But she'd accepted this job along with consequences, and she knew what would happen if she failed.

Still... she prayed to any power out there that she was wrong, that the evidence would lead her somewhere else, that her mind was deceiving her.

She didn't want it to be Alan.

7

Part of her didn't want to go home, because her mother and Maryanne would have questions. Emily would too, when she arrived. She didn't want to tell anyone. Not until she was certain. She didn't want anyone to jump to conclusions. It was too important to get this right. If she was wrong... an innocent man would die and there would be more bodies in the coming days.

In the end, she did go home, and found Maryanne watching a baking show in the living room.

"You okay?" She asked.

"I... don't know. I'll let you know in a bit," Cora replied, heading upstairs. Thankfully, Maryanne didn't follow her.

The first thing she did was go back to the database, pulling up Alan's file again. He wore contacts to hide his true eye colour, and she'd never seen him without them. They made a surprising amount of difference in a person's appearance. There were no medical records from the last few days, let alone the last few months, nothing about him going to the doctor for any injury. She swallowed hard and dug a little deeper. She found the incident with the children, found the files to go with it. It was recommended that he step back from dealing with ghosts for a while.

There was nothing about an address in Toronto. His records went from Edmonton to Winnipeg, and then to St John's. With shaking hands, she picked up her phone to call her sister. Alan was good with computers. Good enough to find out when people wouldn't be home, possibly good enough to change his own records just enough that he'd be overlooked by investigators.

"Everything okay?" Lily asked when she answered.

Cora hesitated.

"Cora?"

She swallowed hard. This was a step toward someone's death.

And saving many other people.

"Do you guys still keep hard copies of people's files?"

"What do you need? There's a good chance they won't be up to the minute, but everyone updates at least once a week. The digital files are more accurate."

"How long ago was it printed?" If it had been done after he arrived, it likely wouldn't have anything about Toronto.

"After he arrived," she replied. "Why?"

"Can you check to see if there's anything about Alan's time in Toronto?"

"He lived in Toronto? He's never mentioned it. I thought he lived in Winnipeg before moving here."

"I know. He said he lived in Toronto for a few years, but the digital file says Winnipeg." And she didn't think he'd get that mixed up. There was only one reason that made this situation make sense, and she didn't like it.

"Weird. I'll see if there's an archived version. Hang on a sec."

"Okay."

"How's the healing going?"

"Alright. I'll probably lie down for a while later."

"Sounds like a good plan." There was a long moment where the only sound was Lilly typing. "Well, fuck... the file was changed a year ago, just before he moved here. But he did live in Toronto, not that far from Cyrus."

"Damn..." It was definitely not looking good.

"But the bodies from Toronto only stop a few weeks ago... why did he change his killing ground?"

"Maybe using the tears to go such a long distance finally got to him. Or he needed to be close to salt water for a new method of reanimation." She tapped her fingers on the desk. "Don't update his file, but send the archived file to Lady Morrigan and highlight the discrepancies."

"Wow, look at you, sounding all official and giving orders."

"Lilly..."

"I'm still allowed to tease, Cora. I'm proud of you. I'll get the file to her."

She felt warmth rush to her face. "Thanks."

Lilly hesitated. "What happens now?"

"I have to kill him?" The words were barely a whisper. "I'll have to call Lady Morrigan and let her know that we found the necromancer first, but I have to kill him." Everything pointed to Alan. She remembered the way he kept pulling his sweater higher around his neck, and the makeup.

"Okay. Is there anything else I can do to help?"

"Nothing right now. Please don't tell Mom or Dad, or anyone else."

"Cora, you're hurt. Do you really expect to take him on your own?"

"He's injured too, even worse than I am."

"Cora..."

"Please trust me. I'm sure about this."

"Okay. Be careful."

"I will." She ended the call and ran a hand through her hair, just taking a minute to take everything in. She couldn't deny the evidence. The phone started ringing, the sound crashing through the silence of her office, startling her. When she saw Stephanie's number, she frowned.

"Hello?"

"Cora? It's Stephanie. Have you heard from Jet today? He left early this morning and hasn't answered any of my calls or texts."

"No, I haven't. I'll try calling him. Might be he just needs some space." She tried to sound optimistic.

"Okay... it's just not like him. But I guess I haven't been around when a close friend of his was murdered." There was a wry, humourless edge to her voice. "I'm probably interrupting your investigation. I'm sorry."

"No, it's fine. Have you tried Mom or Dad? They're keeping pretty close tabs on him right now."

"Neither of them answered when I called. I'll try again, thanks."

"No worries."

"How are your injuries? I dropped by at the hospital, but you were unconscious."

"I'll be feeling them for a while, but I'll recover," she replied.

"Alright. Good luck with your investigation, I'll leave you alone now." But she sounded worried.

Thanks, bye." Cora hung up. Another thing to worry about. She called Jet, but there was no answer, so she sent him a message. Assuming her brother's fiancée would call their parents, she turned her mind back to the problem at hand. She felt like she needed one more thing, one more piece of evidence that would prove to her that Alan was guilty. Or rather, she needed one thing that would mean he wasn't the guilty one.

Rubbing at her aching arm, she realized that there was one more stone to turn over. Alan had claimed to be in Alberta when she was injured because of a family emergency. It wasn't in his records, which didn't mean much at this point. But it did mean that he could have an alibi. If he was really there when she'd been attacked beyond the Veil, that would mean he was innocent. But if she called, that would tip them off, and they might do something that would warn Alan she was closing in on him, which would probably cause him to go after her or someone she cared about. But this could be her last chance to prove his innocence.

She picked up her phone and called the number listed for his parents.

"Hello?" A man's voice answered.

"Hi, can I speak to Gerald Dearil?" She asked, taking a guess at who was on the other end.

"Speaking."

Her mind worked fast to come up with a lie. "I'm Cora Morrigan, a friend of Alan's."

He cut her off before she could get anything else out. "You're the investigator on the necromancer case."

She swallowed hard. "Yes."

"Why are you calling us?" His tone told her that he knew why, he just didn't want to believe it.

"I'm trying to verify the whereabouts of every reaper with ties to Newfoundland three days ago." It was still a lie, but close enough to the truth that it sounded convincing. "Alan isn't active, so his file hasn't been cleared yet."

"Ah, well, as far as we know he's stayed in St John's."

Cora felt like she was going to throw up. "That's all I needed to know, thanks."

"Does that help clear him?"

It was almost impossible to speak. "It helps." Just not in the way he wanted it to.

"Okay. Goodbye." He hung up before she could say anything else. Cora put the phone down and put her head in her hands as her last hope flickered and went out. After days of things moving at a sluggish pace, everything felt like it was going at the speed of light, and she didn't know if she was ready. But she didn't have a choice. She picked up the phone again and called Lady Morrigan, tapping her fingers nervously against her desk.

"You're certain?" The old woman demanded at the news, her tone sharp. Cora understood. If she was wrong... but she wasn't. She was certain of that.

"I am. All of the evidence points to Alan Dearil."

There was a soft sigh on the other end of the line, and Cora thought she could hear regret in it. "Very well. You know what you have to do. I will inform Lady Dearil and Lord Viduus of this, and we will decide how to tell the others, and the rest of the world."

Cora swallowed hard. "I understand."

"Don't waste any more time. And remember... don't hesitate. Alan has crossed a line that should never be crossed, and this is the only way to end it."

"I understand."

"Good luck." The line went dead again.

Next she called Emily. She had no idea if Alan's parents would call him, but they probably would. And that would lead him right to her and the people she loved.

She answered quickly. "Hey, everything okay?" Cora barely held back a sigh of relief at the sound of her voice.

"Yeah... no. Not really. I know who the necromancer is."

There was a pause. "You okay with that?"

"Not really. But I have to be."

"Okay. Couldn't you get Detective Byrne to deal with it?"

"Not with a reaper. He and anyone he sent would just be murdered. This... this is something only my kind can handle." She hated saying it like that, it made her sound inhuman. "I'm going to deal with it now." Before another body could be left in the harbour. "If you see Alan, run away and call me."

"Jesus Christ."

She managed a hollow laugh. "Not even close."

"Be careful."

"I will."

"Are you going to do this today?"

"It has to be done as soon as possible."

"Okay. If you're gone when I get to your place, I'll see you when you get home." There was a tremor to her voice, a hint of fear.

"Okay."

"I love you."

She hoped the rising dread she felt wasn't a hint of what was to come, that Emily would really arrive at her house safe and sound. "I love you, too." She ended the call, holding the phone in a white-knuckled grip as she tried to quell her panic. The faster Alan was dealt with, the safer everyone would be, especially the people she loved. She just had to look at it that way.

Was that how Alan saw it? The death of the few for the good of the many? Looking back, she had the impression that he saw himself as the hero, especially with their conversation at the university. The tragic figure of a more tragic tale. She felt sick. This wasn't what she was supposed to be doing. She wasn't a murderer, and she didn't want to become one, even though she was now a sanctioned assassin whose mission surpassed laws and morals. What would she do if she ever saw his family? Would they hate her for what she'd done? Or would they thank her for stopping him? She truly didn't know which would be worse.

How did one murder another human? Cora had to figure that out. There were so many ways, some fast, some slow. She had no desire to torture. She just wanted this done and over with as fast as possible.

She had no gun, and no way to get one. The detective did... but she couldn't let him take charge. This was her job. Alan was her responsibility. Still... she should let them know the case would soon be closed. But wouldn't it be better to deal with it first, then let them know? She didn't know. And she was procrastinating.

She wasn't ready for this. She didn't want to do this. She looked at her phone. How the fuck was she going to organize a murder ambush? But she didn't want a murder in her home, as weird as that sounded for a reaper. Would she try to find an excuse to go to his home? She couldn't do it in public. What would she say?

Her best option was probably to wait until he was done at work, then call and make up some excuse to go to his place. Then kill him. She felt like she was going to throw up.

Instead, she tried calling her brother again. There was still no answer. She sent another text, and narrowly resisted the urge to call Emily again. She didn't want to seem paranoid. She needed to figure this out, and she was the only one who could, but she didn't want to be alone. Agitated, she stood and went downstairs. Maryanne got up as soon as she saw Cora's face.

"What's wrong?"

"I hate this," she replied, starting to pace and raking her fingers through her hair. "I hate everything about this. I'm *certain* it's Alan... but I want to find something to prove me wrong. I... I called Lady Morrigan. She gave me the clear to... execute him." The word almost got stuck in her throat.

Maryanne closed the distance between them and hugged her. Since Cora was a reaper, she could physically touch ghosts. She hugged Maryanne back, her body shaking.

"I'm sorry you have to do this," she said. "But I know you can do it. You're strong, Cora."

"I'm sorry too." Her phone rang upstairs, and she was tempted to ignore it, but couldn't. Not at a time like this. She ran upstairs, but it was a message from Emily, that she'd be longer running errands than she'd thought. Cora sent a quick reply and took her phone downstairs with her. She made it to the bottom of the stairs when it rang again.

It was Alan.

"Hello?" She tried to keep her tone even.

"Cora, I need you to come to the Queen's Road house." His voice was low and urgent. She didn't need to ask which house he meant.

Dread was a lead weight in her stomach. "What happened?"

"It's your brother... I think he's going to try to resurrect Cyrus."

That wasn't what she'd expected to hear. He had Jet? Was that why her brother wasn't answering his phone? No. Jet was too good to be caught. He knew to be careful, he was an amazing fighter. "I'll be right over."

"Good. Hurry." The line went dead.

Heart racing, she tried to call Jet again, but there was no answer. Stephanie's line was busy, and so were her parents' phones. Would he have really taken her brother? She'd spent so much time worried about Emily... but then, maybe Alan lied. Or maybe he knew Emily was the obvious target. Her mind was racing and she had to calm down. She turned around to go get her knife and ran downstairs.

"Cora?"

"I need you to call Mom, Dad, Lilly, and Stephanie. Find out if any of them know where Jet is," she replied, trying to get her shit together. "And make sure you know where Emily is." She couldn't eliminate the possibility that he would lie to her.

"Oh God..." Maryanne jumped to the right conclusion.

"I'm going to the Queen's Road house to kill Alan." If he wanted her there, she had no doubt he'd be waiting.

"Do I tell them what's going on?" She was much quicker to get it together.

"Yes." She didn't hesitate. "I'm going to call Mike on the way."

Maryanne nodded. "Good luck."

Cora was going to need it.

She called the detective on the way to the house, but it went through to voicemail. She let him know what was happening, and reminded him to stay out of the fight, and preferably outside the house. If a normal person stepped through the tear, even by accident, they would die in seconds without a reaper's protection. She put her phone on silent after that, so she wouldn't forget later.

Heart in her throat, she pushed the speed limit as much as she dared in the old, winding streets of downtown St John's, every slow driver fraying her nerves further, every red light making her heart race faster. She parked with more expedience than care as close as she could get, ignoring the blaring horn as someone nearly took the door off her car while she rushed out and up to the front door.

The house had always possessed a strange, slightly creepy energy, even more than other places where the tear in the Veil couldn't be closed. She drew her dagger and angled her body to hide it as she reached for the door, very carefully turning the knob. It wasn't locked. She left it closed and looked around. There was no sign of Jet's car, and she couldn't remember what Alan drove. But that didn't matter, did it? Why didn't the security system go off? Unless he really did have Jet and had forced him to reveal the codes... but if he'd been there before, he'd likely seen the code entered, and could have remembered it.

She pulled out her phone. There was a missed call and voicemail from Mike that she ignored, and nothing from her family or Stephanie. Nothing from Emily. A text from Mike appeared, letting her know that he was on the way with backup.

In a last-ditch attempt to put her mind at ease before she had to fight for her life and to kill another human being, she called her brother one more time.

It rang. Once. Twice. She could barely breathe.

There was an answer.

"Cora, he threw his phone on the ground, it keeps ringing but he refuses to talk to anyone. You have to hurry!"

Alan had her brother's phone.

Alan had her brother.

A strange mix of panic and determination gripped her heart and mind as she opened the door and stepped in, hyper-aware of everything around her. She knew the house, she'd been there a thousand times before. She knew exactly where the tear was. Alan was most likely there. She went to the panel that controlled the alarm system. It had been disarmed, and she tried not to let that get to her. She pressed the panic button that didn't set off the alarm. It would send an alert to the security company and they would make damn sure to contact her mother or father, and then her mother would come to the house. Just in case something happened, in case she lost... there would still be someone who could arrive quickly and finish the job.

"Alan?" She called out, shutting the door audibly. She needed to try to play ignorant as long as possible.

"Downstairs! Hurry!"

Whether she was ready or not, this was the end.

8

"Alan?" She called out again as she shut and locked the door behind her. Mike and his officers wouldn't be able to just barge in. She looked around, tense and ready for anything. She could feel the energy of the tear, prickling against her skin like thousands of pins and needles. That was in the basement, and that was likely where she would find Alan, so she headed down the stairs.

Alan was there, standing in front of the thick silver line that marked the tear, its ethereal glow lighting up the room. "Good, you're here. He went through." Alan was still wearing contacts, putting on a panicked act. "He wouldn't listen to me."

"How long ago?" She just had to get close. Then she could stab him and end this. She took a few steps toward him when she got to the bottom of the stairs, not quite within his reach, but close enough.

"Maybe ten minutes? He called me and was asking a bunch of strange questions because I was helping you with the investigation. I eventually got him to talk to me and raced over. I called you as soon as I got here." He raked a hand through his hair and looked at her, his expression stark. "Cora... what if he's the necromancer? What if it was him all along?"

She took a chance and lunged as he turned his head toward the tear again, but he jumped out of the way. Alan stared at her for a moment, clutching his injured side. His expression of shock and betrayal slowly hardened when he saw that she knew what was going on.

"Where is my brother?" She demanded, lunging again. She could hear sirens approaching in the distance.

"Right where I left him," Alan replied, taking a step back and to the side to dodge her. "If you're quick you should be able to save him before any real damage is done. Just let me go and let me continue my work. It's almost done. I almost have it figured out"

"But you're murdering people, Alan. You're taking lives and you're trapping souls!"

"So I can bring them back!" He replied, desperation and guilt twisting his expression. "I can fix it. I can bring them back. I just need a little more time and then I'll have it. I found spells in ancient documents. I just need to get the placement right for the flow of power to give life back to the body."

Her heart was breaking for him, because she was sure that he absolutely did believe that. But it was *not possible*. "What about Cyrus? You *destroyed* his soul. There's nothing left!" It wouldn't do any good to argue about the impossibility of what he wanted to do. He was too far gone.

Alan ran a hand over his face, wiping away the makeup he'd used to conceal the darkened veins at his temples. He saw where her eyes went and turned his head so she couldn't see them as easily. "He left me with no choice, and I'll have to live with that for the rest of my life." He sounded sincere. "But he died for the greater good, just like you and your brother will unless you let me go!" The guilt and regret were written all over his face, but she could see that his mind was made up. He lunged at her and she ducked, trying to get her blade up into his stomach. All she managed to do was slice open his shirt before he kicked her, sending her stumbling into the tear.

It was like plunging into a bucket of ice. It was so cold it felt like her skin was burning. She gasped for breath, the air thin even as it threatened to freeze her lungs. She held her blade ready and took a step back away from the tear, almost tripping over something. She looked down. It was some*one*.

"Jet!" She knelt beside him and struggled to find his pulse. It was there, but it felt fast and shallow. Heart in her throat, she tried to shake him awake. He was so cold, and his hair... once it had been as dark as hers, but now it was almost snow white. How long had he been here? It had to be longer than ten minutes. "Jet, wake up! Please! Jet!" Her voice echoed strangely here, the way a ghost's voice would on the other side of the Veil. Jet stirred slightly but didn't open his eyes.

"I drugged him." She turned her head to see Alan but didn't turn her body. "Just let me go, Cora, and I'll let you take him and leave alive. Or better, help me. If we can finish my work, we'll be able to save everyone. We won't have to escort any more children across the Veil."

She swallowed hard. A plan was forming in her mind. "Alan, the dead can't come back to life. It's not possible."

"They can! There has to be a way! Just think about it, Cora. I know you're smart. If we can just jumpstart the chemical processes that keep the body working long enough, we can put the soul back in and it will keep the body going again. Our magic keeps us in better shape for longer, it lets us cross the Veil. We should be able to shape that power and use it! The mystical sigils will hold and direct the power, like they do on our daggers!" She stayed low, moving slowly until her body hid her brother's dagger. Like her own, it was hung from his belt. As Alan kept talking, she drew with her her left hand, keeping both hands out of his direct line of sight. Jet's dagger felt wrong in her hand, both because it was his dagger and because it had been made specifically for his hand. Right now, though, that didn't matter. It was sharp.

"Nothing you do is ever going to bring them back!" She snapped, breaking him out of his rant. "You *murdered* them. You stole their lives, and nothing will *ever* fix that!"

He stared at her for a moment. "You're just like everyone else, aren't you? You don't understand. Just like none of them understood. I see that now." He was eerily calm, and it frightened her. "I'm sorry, Cora. I didn't want to do this." He lunged at her, blade poised to end her life. Cora moved to the side, feigning a strike at his outstretched arm while she sank Jet's blade into his calf. She twisted it and tore it free as Alan screamed and stumbled. She ignored the pain that shot through her injured arm, instead jumping to her feet and stabbing him through the heart before he could recover.

Alan stared at her, shocked. "Cora..."

Tears blurred her vision as she twisted the dagger to make sure she killed him. She felt more than saw his body go limp before it slid to the ground, lifeless. Dead.

Cora wiped her eyes on her sleeve and shoved her dagger back into its sheath before turning to Jet. Alan's body would vanish into nothing if left alone, but she had more important concerns. She put Jet's dagger back. Cora would happily sit through his ranting about the blood in the sheath as long as he lived. He was heavy, and she could only use one arm to drag him. But she managed, pulling him out of the rift just as the detective came running down the stairs, followed by her mother.

"I'll get the paramedics!" Mike said, changing course as Cora's mother reached them. She immediately knelt by Jet, checking for a pulse.

"Is he going to be okay?" Cora's voice cracked.

"I don't know," was the worrying reply. "Where's Alan?"

She pointed at the tear.

For a moment she could see grief on her mother's face, but that was replaced by something harder. "Good." He'd acted like a friend to their family this whole time.

Everything became a blur after that. Somehow, she ended up at St. Claire's hospital, blankets wrapped around her as she sat in the waiting area with her father and sister. Only one person was allowed in with Jet at the moment. There was talk of sending him to Halifax or Montreal, where there were reapers who'd become doctors, specifically to help thier kind with injuries and problems that resulted from their work.

She'd killed someone. She was a murderer.

At one point, Mike pulled her aside to find out what happened. She couldn't really remember what he asked, or what he had her fill out. Somehow, she found herself seated next to her father again. Next came the news that Jet was being moved to Halifax, which set off more chaos, more confusion. Her parents went with her brother, while Lilly took her home, where Emily and Maryanne were waiting. As soon as they were in through the door Emily pulled Cora into her arms, holding her tight. Cora could only cling to her as everything finally started to sink in. She'd killed someone. She wasn't supposed to kill people, she was supposed to help those who were lost. Alan had been lost, but there had been nothing she could do. Right?

Doubts swirled in her mind. Would it have been possible to bring him around? To fix things? To make him understand? Even though she knew it wasn't possible. Everything had been tried with previous necromancers. He would have been dead in a few months even if she hadn't put a blade in his heart. The darkening veins were a sign.

So many people tried to congratulate her, to tell her that she'd done a good job. Or a necessary one. She wanted to scream. It wasn't right. Why were they celebrating? Even Mike didn't seem to understand. Not in the way she did. Alan had died, but it felt like a part of her had died as well. But she couldn't quite put her finger on it. They'd taught her how to fight and defend herself, how to handle ghosts and poltergeists. She'd killed them before, but that was different in a way she couldn't quite wrap her head around. Alan had been a living, breathing person, not a lost soul that lingered too long after death. This was different, wasn't it? Should it be? She felt conflicted, but also felt like she shouldn't feel conflicted because she knew better. She knew there was only one answer, she knew there was only one way to stop it. She supposed she would just have to learn to live with it, like others before her had done.

Lady Morrigan, at least, seemed unsurprised, and had asked outright if Cora felt such doubts when she called.

"What you're feeling is normal, Cora. I've seen this happen three times before in my life, and every time the reaper felt the same after. Two of them are still alive. I will see if they're able to talk to you. Its not something either of them talk about, but I think they'll make an exception," she said. She didn't bother to try to turn it into some kind of victory, because it wasn't. Not really. Not with so many victims, not with two of their own dead, and another in critical condition.

"Thank you," she said.

"Get some rest now," she instructed.

"Yes, Lady Morrigan," Cora replied as the call ended, even though she didn't see how she could rest at all.

The chaos didn't end after she went home. There didn't seem to be an end in sight. The case was all over the news, everywhere she looked. The names of the victims were starting to be made public0, families appearing on television. They tried to dissect Alan as they did all serial killers, but the reapers refused to talk, refused to share any more details than absolutely necessary while they all mourned the tragedy. When she left the house, people stared even when she had her sunglasses on. There was no hiding and no separating her name from any of it.

There were also reports to be written and sent to the family heads involved. But first, the matter of the souls that Alan had trapped and getting a final count of his victims. Luckily, Alan had kept the souls close. Though it was disturbing to see a closet full of lead-lined jars in his apartment.

"Fuck..." Lilly murmured as they took in the sight. Each one was carefully labelled with the victim's name, a date, an address, and map coordinates. "Did that bastard record where he killed them and where he put the bodies?"

"He was a researcher. You have to keep track of everything." It was a terrible excuse for a joke, and Cora didn't try to hide it.

"Maybe... do you think this is all of them?"

"Lady Morrigan said that if we found one of them, we'd likely find them all. Apparently, necromancers like to keep them close. You know, in case they succeed. Then they can fix what they did."

"Okay." She pulled out a pad of paper and a pen. "It seems almost cruel not to let them say goodbye to their families."

"I know... but some of them might have gone mad or become poltergeists after being trapped like this." While ghosts appeared at the size the person had been in life, they could be compacted into tiny jars. From her understanding, it was fairly traumatic.

"Right. Line them up. I'll record them and then you can release them?"

Cora nodded and started carefully taking down the jars and putting them on a table so Lilly could write the information down. By the dates on the jars, he'd been doing this for two years, though at first there could be months between victims instead of days. They worked in a steady rhythm, Cora ignoring the growing ache in her wounded arm and side. The jars weren't heavy or fragile, but she still treated them as such, knowing what they contained. At least families would be able to get some kind of closure now, as awful as it would be. But that wasn't her job.

"That's the last of them," she said when she put down the last jar with a name. There were others, blank and waiting, on the bottom shelf. Lilly nodded, and Cora drew her dagger. She'd cleaned it, along with Jet's, and sharpened it, working until the steel shone mirror-bright. But in her mind she could still see Alan's blood dripping down the blade.

She wondered if the image would ever go away.

Taking a deep breath, she focused, feeling for the division between this world and the next, the Veil. She raised her blade and cut cleanly through it, ethereal silver light spilling into the room. Picking up the first jar, she moved it close to the tear and opened the lid. There was a flicker of light, and the soul vanished inside. She put the jar back on the table and moved on to the next.

"Our total for living victims is forty-six, including Cyrus," Lilly said when the last soul had been freed. "I don't know how many ghosts he killed, and I don't think we'll ever know."

Cora thought of Will again, who had died trying to protect her. "Yeah..." She swallowed hard and shut the tear. There was a surprising amount of resistance, but she managed, and then sank into a chair, aware of her sister watching her closely.

"You okay?"

Cora shrugged and pulled out her phone. "Mom says that some of our cousins are coming in from Halifax to watch the tear tonight." She ran a hand over her face. "I completely forgot it's Halloween."

Lilly frowned for a moment. "Shit, you're right. Well..." She looked down at the list. "I don't think I'll be doing much this year. Did she say anything about Jet?"

She looked back down at the message. "He's sleeping right now, but he'll be out in a few days." Jet would mostly recover, but there were doubts on whether he'd be able to deal with ghosts. While Cora had managed to get him back through the Veil just in time, if he crossed over again either in soul or body, he would die. In the meantime, their mother would take over monitoring the Queen's Road tear. It had been calm the last few days, luckily, but Halloween was never calm. She just wanted to go home, curl up with Emily, and sleep for a week.

"That's good." Lilly looked around. "Is his family coming to deal with his stuff?"

"I don't know. I would assume they are? Lady Morrigan said they were flying in sometime this week." She didn't want to be there anymore. She had murdered the man that lived here. Even though she knew there would be no ghost, it felt haunted. "I don't think there's anything else we need to do here."

"Okay, we can go." Lilly handed her the papers with the information and they left, locking the door behind them. "Why don't you get in the car and I'll return these to the landlord?" Alan's keys had vanished with his body. But Cora hadn't thought of that at the time. She'd just wanted to stop Alan and save her brother. She didn't fight her sister and just headed for the car, replying to her mother's message so she wouldn't have to look at anyone. Her picture was in the paper, on the news, and all over the internet as the reaper who'd killed the necromancer. It almost sounded like there was a joke in there somewhere, but she couldn't find it. The worst part was that she could understand why Alan did it. She could understand the frustration, the desire to reverse the unfairness of life. But that wasn't possible.

The drive home was mostly silent, and when they got back Cora was surprised to see Emily's car in the driveway. She knew Emily had the day off, but had figured she'd be out, or at her own home.

"Are you going to be alright?" Lilly asked as she pulled in by the end of the driveway.

Cora managed a weak smile. "Eventually. It's just... a lot."

"Yeah, I get it." She reached over and hugged her, careful of her injured arm. "Go, eat too much candy. I won't tell Mom."

Her smile was a little stronger as she finally pulled away. "No, Jet was the one who tattled. You were too busy bribing me so I wouldn't tell on *you*."

"And as far as I can see you have nothing to complain about."

"Right." Cora got out and waved as Lilly drove off, then headed inside. There were paint cans by the door. She sighed as she took off her boots, wondering what colour change she would come home to in the next week as she stepped into the living room.

"Hey, how was... everything?" Emily struggled for the right word as she stood and walked over, wrapping her arms around Cora. She leaned against her, slipping her arms around her waist.

"Not great," she replied honestly, hiding her face against Emily's shirt. "There were so many of them..." And she was certain at least two had become poltergeists, judging on the way they'd left the jars. "But it's almost over. Just the reports for the family heads and Detective Byrne's people." Hopefully she wouldn't have to cross the Veil again any time soon.

"Okay. I'm here for you, and I'm not going anywhere," Emily promised. At least one good thing was happening, because this time, Cora believed her.

About the Author

Stacey Oakley lives in Newfoundland enjoying the weather that most people hate. She has a BA in Art History &Visual Studies and a post-grad diploma in Cultural Resource Management from the University of Victoria and is working on a diploma in Executive Office Administration from the College of the North Atlantic. When not explaining what those mean or studying, she can usually be found reading a book or writing one. So far she has published two short stories and a novel, *Hunter's Soul.*

www.ingramcontent.com/pod-product-compliance
Lightning Source LLC
Chambersburg PA
CBHW071535100726
47908CB00004B/1404